喚醒你的英文語感！

Get a Feel for English !

英文多角片語建構

作者 / 白安竹
Andrew E. Bennett

CONTENTS

Chapter 3 · Money & Shopping 金錢與購物

Chapter 4 · Challenges 挑戰

Chapter 5 · Daily Life 日常生活

本書使用方法

一、準備多益測驗與提升英語實力同時進行

本書大部分的主題，與多益測驗的頻考主題相符，是準備多益考試者可以充分利用的片語學習書。但是必須強調的是，本書絕對不只能幫助考試，而是能讓讀者真正學會使用英文。

二、規劃1個月（30天）的學習份量，方便讀者控管學習進度。

每一課的內容都包含了：有趣的情境對話、5個核心片語與例句、進階解析文法與用法、3則句型練習、練習題。

須要花費的時間因人而異，大約在30分鐘到1個小時左右。如果想要反覆的聽MP3作聽力與口說練習，可能會需要更多時間，但是這樣的練習對讀者開口說英文有相當大的幫助，同時也能準備多益考試的聽力測驗。

本書的核心片語共有150個，數量不多，但是只要能夠發揮這些核心片語的力量，必然對英語實力的提升更有成效。

三、善用每個小單元，多層次學習片語，達到最高學習成效

Step 1 → 從情境對話開始接觸片語

和文章或例句比起來，「對話」是我們接觸外語最簡單的方式。因為有前後文和情境能幫助我們了解意思，而且又不像文章的句子那麼長。每一課有一篇精選的情境對話，篇幅都不長，而且有故事性，所以一次讀完也不會有壓力。

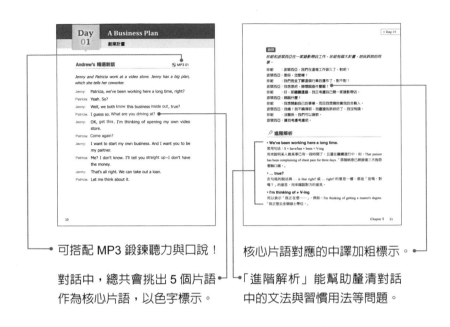

可搭配 MP3 鍛鍊聽力與口說！

對話中，總共會挑出 5 個片語
作為核心片語，以色字標示。

核心片語對應的中譯加粗標示。

「進階解析」能幫助釐清對話
中的文法與習慣用法等問題。

Step 2 → 將對話中的 5 個核心片語做延伸學習

有別於前面情境對話的句子，此處
列出不同的例句或短對話，能更透
徹的學習同一個片語。

可搭配 MP3 聽例句！

「進階查詢」透過對片語的來源或用法
的說明，幫助讀者更輕鬆記憶。

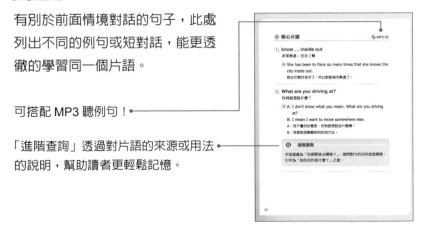

Step 3 → 補充精挑句型，學習再加廣

情境對話中，除了核心片語之外，作者還設計了實用句型在其中。「精挑句型」將句型學習再加廣，列出可替換語詞，提供讀者練習，成為能自然出口的口袋好用句。

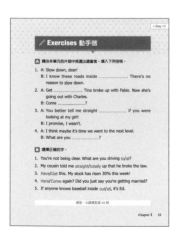

Step 4 → Exercises 動手做，透過對題目思考的過程來加深學習的印象。

每一課的尾聲都是大約九題填充或選字題，在這裡可以再次複習片語，並且從不同的例句複習片語。

本書作者是來自哈佛大學的教育專家，同時也是語言學習經驗非常豐富的實踐者！除了母語英文之外，他精通中文、日文、西班牙文、法文、德文。因此，由作者親力撰寫的獨門學習專欄是最有說服力的！讀者可以從中找到適合自己的學習方法與秘訣，您的語言學習將事半功倍。

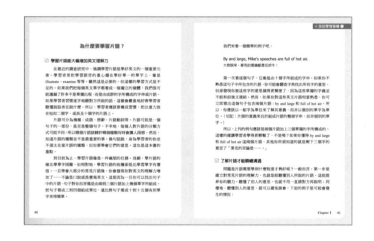

Chapter 1

Business 業務

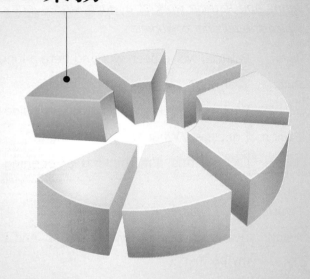

英語學習專欄 ① 為什麼要學習片語？

Andrew's 精選對話　　　　　　　　　　　🔊 MP3 01

Jenny and Patricia work at a video store. Jenny has a big plan, which she tells her coworker.

Jenny:　Patricia, we've been working here a long time, right?

Patricia:　Yeah. So?

Jenny:　Well, we both know this business inside out, true?

Patricia:　I guess so. What are you driving at?

Jenny:　OK, get this. I'm thinking of opening my own video store.

Patricia:　Come again?

Jenny:　I want to start my own business. And I want you to be my partner.

Patricia:　Me? I don't know. I'll tell you straight up—I don't have the money.

Jenny:　That's all right. We can take out a loan.

Patricia:　Let me think about it.

翻譯

珍妮和派翠西亞在一家錄影帶店工作，珍妮有個大計畫，她告訴她的同事。

珍妮　　：派翠西亞，我們在這裡工作很久了，對吧？
派翠西亞：是呀，怎麼樣？
珍妮　　：我們**完全了解**這個行業的運作了，對不對？
派翠西亞：我想是吧，**妳想說些什麼呢**？
珍妮　　：好，那**聽聽這個**，我正考慮自己開一家錄影帶店。
派翠西亞：**妳說什麼？**
珍妮　　：我想開創自己的事業，而且我想請妳當我的合夥人。
派翠西亞：我嗎？我不曉得耶，我**直接**告訴妳好了，我沒有錢。
珍妮　　：沒關係，我們可以貸款。
派翠西亞：讓我考慮考慮吧。

📌 進階解析

• We've been working here a long time.

常用句法：S + have/has + been + V-ing
用來說明某人做某事已有一段時間了，且還在繼續進行中，如：That patient has been complaining of chest pain for three days. 「那個病患已經接連三天抱怨著胸口痛。」

• ... true?

在句尾的說法與 ... is that right? 或 ... right? 的意思一樣，都是「是嗎，對嗎？」的意思，用來確認對方的意見。

• I'm thinking of + V-ing

用以表示「我正在想……」，例如：I'm thinking of getting a master's degree. 「我正想去念個碩士學位。」

① **know ... inside out**

非常熟悉；完全了解

例 She has been to Paris so many times that she knows the city inside out.

她去巴黎好多次了，所以對那城市熟透了。

② **What are you driving at?**

你到底想說什麼？

例 A: I don't know what you mean. What are you driving at?

B: I mean I want to move somewhere else.

A：我不懂你的意思，你到底想說些什麼啊？

B：我是說我要搬到別的地方去。

🔍 **進階查詢**

字面意義為「你要開車去哪裡？」，詢問對方的目的地是哪裡，引申為「你的目的是什麼？」之意。

③ Get this.

聽聽看。

例 Get this. The newspaper says someone's building a hotel in space!

你聽聽看這個，報紙說有人要在太空中蓋旅館！

④ Come again?

你說什麼；再說一次。

例 A: I want to shave off all my hair.

B: Come again?

A：我想剃光頭。

B：你再說一次。

⑤ straight up

直接

例 Give me the bad news straight up.

直接告訴我壞消息吧。

☑ 精挑句型

綠字部分為替換語詞，你也可以試著加上更多適當的替換字詞。

①

I'm thinking of opening my own	video store. restaurant. coffee shop.

我正考慮自己開一家錄影帶店。／餐廳。／咖啡店。

②

I want to	start my own business. be my own boss. go into business for myself.

我想開創自己的事業。／自己當老闆。／自己創業。

③

I don't have the	money. cash. capital.

我沒有錢。／現金。／資金。

✏ Exercises 動手做

A 請由本單元的片語中挑選出適當者，填入下列空格。

1. A: Slow down, dear!

   B: I know these roads inside _____. There's no reason to slow down.

2. A: Get _____. Tina broke up with Fabio. Now she's going out with Charles.

   B: Come _____?

3. A: You better tell me straight _____ if you were looking at my girl!

   B: I promise, I wasn't.

4. A: I think maybe it's time we went to the next level.

   B: What are you _____?

B 選擇正確的字。

1. You're not being clear. What are you driving to/at?

2. My cousin told me straight/totally up that he broke the law.

3. Have/Get this. My stock has risen 30% this week!

4. Here/Come again? Did you just say you're getting married?

5. If anyone knows baseball inside out/all, it's Ed.

解答、中譯請見第 222 頁

Andrew's 精選對話   ◉ MP3 03

Months ago, Robert and Arlene decided to start a computer company together. Now their business, New World, is finally open.

Arlene: We've actually done it. But it hasn't been a cakewalk.

Robert: I'll say. I've been so busy the last three months I haven't had time to breathe.

Arlene: That makes two of us. Now it's time for us to make a fortune!

Robert: That's the spirit! Let's open that bottle of champagne and celebrate!

Arlene: OK. I propose a toast to years and years of New World's success.

Robert: To our success! May our business prosper and go public soon, so we can get rich off the IPO!

Arlene: Well said. Good luck, partner.

Robert: Good luck!

翻譯

幾個月前，羅伯特和阿蓮決定一起開電腦公司，現在他們的事業，新世界，終於開張了。

阿蓮　　：我們終於辦到了，不過，**真不容易啊**。

羅伯特：**我同意**，過去三個月來我真的忙翻了，**忙到連呼吸的時間都沒有**。

阿蓮　　：**我也一樣**，現在該是我們賺錢的時候了！

羅伯特：**就是這個精神**！我們開那瓶香檳來慶祝吧！

阿蓮　　：我提議乾一杯，祝新世界連年成功。

羅伯特：祝我們成功！希望我們的事業可以蓬勃發展而且股票趕快上市，這樣我們就可以在公司一上市就變成有錢人了。

阿蓮　　：說得好。祝我們好運，合夥人。

羅伯特：祝我們好運！

進階解析

• a toast

「乾杯」的意思，若要說為了什麼乾杯，可以用 a toast to + N/Ving，如 a toast to your health「為你的健康而乾杯」。

• get rich off the IPO

從哪裡致富或賺錢可以用 get rich off + N 或 make money off + N。IPO 為 Initial Public Offering 的縮寫，意為「股票首度公開發行」。

• Well said.

即為「說得好」，同樣的用法還有 Well done.「做得好」。

① **It hasn't been a cakewalk.**

這是不容易的事。

例 A: Is your training at the academy difficult?

B: It hasn't been a cakewalk, that's for sure.

A：你在學院裡的訓練困難嗎？

B：當然不容易啊。

② **I'll say.**

我同意。

例 A: Something needs to be done about the pollution in this city.

B: I'll say.

A：這個城市裡的污染得想辦法解決。

B：我同意。

③ **I haven't had time to breathe.**

我非常忙碌（忙到沒時間喘息）。

例 Putting this play together has been so demanding that I haven't had time to breathe.

要完成這齣戲是件大工程，我真的忙翻了。

④ **That makes two of us.**

我的處境（或感覺）跟你一樣。

例 A: It's such a beautiful day outside. I wish I could go to the beach.

B: That makes two of us.

A：今天外面的天氣真好，我真希望去海邊。

B：我也有同樣的感覺。

> **Q** 進階查詢
>
> 意思是「我們兩個人的情況一樣；我跟你處在同樣狀況」，這個句子也可以是 three/four/five ... of us「我們三 / 四 / 五……人都處在同樣的狀況」。

⑤ **That's the spirit.**

就是這種精神；精神可嘉。

例 That's the spirit. Keep thinking positive thoughts, and you'll do fine.

就是這種精神，保持正面的思維，你就會做得很好。

☑ 精挑句型

綠字部分為替換語詞，你也可以試著加上更多適當的替換字詞。

①

We	actually finally really	did it.

我們真的／終於／真的辦到了。

②

Now it's time for us to	make a fortune! rise to the top. earn some money.

現在該是我們賺大錢／攀上顛峰／賺些錢的時候了。

③

I propose a toast to	years and years of New World's success. your health, wealth, and happiness. the newest member of our club.

我提議舉杯祝新世界連年成功。／祝你健康、富有、快樂。／歡迎我們俱樂部的新會員。

✎ Exercises 動手做

A 請由本單元的片語中挑選出適當者，填入下列空格。

1. A: I don't care about the latest fashions.
   B: That makes _____.

2. I've been so busy this week that I haven't _____.

3. A: Well, I guess I'll just keep trying.
   B: That's _____!

4. A: Becoming rich and successful is no _____.
   B: I'll _____. It takes a lot of hard work.

B 選擇正確的字。

1. A: This cake is delicious.
   B: I'll/I say. I have to ask Tina for the recipe.

2. A: OK, I'll try one more time.
   B: That's the/a spirit!

3. A: I'm so exhausted that I don't think I can take another step.
   B: That makes/is two of us. What a tough hike!

4. Mary said learning to use that program is no cakerun/cakewalk.

5. Since I started working full-time again, I haven't had/wanted time to breathe.

解答、中譯請見第 222 頁

Andrew's 精選對話

Jacob is considering investing in a new business. He's talking with his friend Betty about his plan.

Jacob: A friend of mine is going to open a hardware store. He wants me to be his partner.

Betty: You don't say. How much do you know about this guy?

Jacob: We met last year at a bowling alley. We play together a few times a month. He seems on the up and up.

Betty: So, he just wants you to give him the money?

Jacob: Not give, invest. He'll give me 20% of his profits for three years.

Betty: That's good, but it may be risky. You might be digging your own grave.

Jacob: I wasn't born yesterday. I know what I'm doing.

Betty: Whatever you say. Just be careful.

Jacob: I will.

翻譯

雅各正考慮要投資一個新的生意，他正和朋友貝蒂談到他的計劃。

雅各：我有一個朋友要開一家賣電腦硬體設備的店，他要我當他的合夥人。

貝蒂：**真的嗎**？你對這個傢伙了解多少？

雅各：我們去年在保齡球球道上認識的，我們一個月會一起打幾次球，他人
看起來蠻**老實的**。

貝蒂：那麼，他只是要你給他錢吧？

雅各：不是給，是投資。他會連續三年給我他獲利的兩成。

貝蒂：那很棒啊，不過有點風險，你很可能是正在**自掘墳墓**。

雅各：**我可不是三歲小孩子**，我知道我在做什麼。

貝蒂：**隨你怎麼說吧**。不過還是小心一點的好。

雅各：我會的。

📌 進階解析

• a bowling alley

指的就是「保齡球的球道」。

• S + seem/seems + adj.

意為「S 看起來似乎……」，例如：Ed seems OK.「艾德看起來似乎不錯。」
或 She seems fine.「她看起來似乎蠻好的。」

• Not give, invest.

其句法為 Not + V, V「不是……，而是……」，此句法經常運用在對話當中。

• You don't say.

意為「真的嗎？」、「是那樣嗎？」。

① **You don't say.**
真的嗎；是那樣嗎？

例 A: A few of us are going camping next week.
B: You don't say.
A：我們有幾個人下星期要去露營。
B：真的嗎？

② **on the up and up**
誠實；老實

例 You can trust that dealer. He's on the up and up.
你可以相信那個生意人，他很誠實的。

③ **dig one's own grave**
自掘墳墓；自己給自己找麻煩

例 This is a risky move you're considering. Be careful not to dig your own grave.
你想採取的這個舉動很冒險，你要小心別給自己找麻煩。

> 🔍 — **進階查詢**
>
> 是指某人在「挖自己的墳墓」，就像是搬石頭砸自己的腳，其舉動會害到自己，中文裡也有「自掘墳墓」這個說法。

④ **I wasn't born yesterday.**

我不是三歲小孩；我有經驗與知識。

例 There's no need to point out the danger. I wasn't born yesterday.

沒有必要把危險指出來，我又不是三歲小孩。

⑤ **Whatever you say.**

隨你怎麼說吧。（我不一定同意）

例 A: One day, I'm going to own my own airplane.

B: Whatever you say.

A：總有一天，我會擁有自己的飛機。

B：隨你怎麼說吧。

☑ 精挑句型

綠字部分為替換語詞,你也可以試著加上更多適當的替換字詞。

①

A friend of mine is going to open a	hardware store. restaurant. bar.

我有一個朋友要開一家賣電腦硬體設備的店。/餐廳。/酒吧。

②

He seems	on the up and up. honest. like a nice guy.

他人看起來蠻老實的。/誠實的。/好的。

③

Just	be careful. watch yourself. try and be cautious.

只不過你還是要小心一點。/你還是要留意一點。/你還是要謹慎一點。

✏ **Exercises** 動手做

▼

A 請由本單元的片語中挑選出適當者，填入下列空格。

1. A: You have to check out a used car carefully before buying it.
   B: I know that. I wasn't _____.
2. A: I could beat you all at poker.
   B: Whatever _____. I'm too poor to challenge you.
3. We have to be careful with our proposal, or we may _____ grave.
4. A: If what they say is on the _____, we'll make a lot of money from this deal.
   B: _____ don't say. That's great.

B 選擇正確的字。

1. A: I could easily beat Michael Jordan one on one.
   B: Whatever/However you say.
2. Are you sure this deal is on the up in/and up?
3. Sheila says she has everything under control, but I'm worried she's filling/digging her own grave.
4. A: I'm getting married in August.
   B: You won't/don't say.
5. A: He might be lying to you.
   B: I wasn't born/here yesterday. I've already thought of that possibility.

解答、中譯請見第 223 頁

Andrew's 精選對話

🎧 MP3 07

Laureen is very excited about one of her investments.

Laureen: Emma, come here. Step on it.

Emma: Hold your horses. I'm coming. What are you so worked up about?

Laureen: OK, remember that stock I bought last year? The one in the small computer company?

Emma: Yeah. What about it?

Laureen: I sold it yesterday for twice as much as I paid for it.

Emma: Right on! How many shares did you have?

Laureen: Ten.

Emma: Ten? Are you sure you made money? What about commission charges?

Laureen: Who cares? Listen, I just bought. fifteen shares in another company. I re-invested my earnings!

Emma: Oh, brother.

翻譯

洛琳對她的一項投資感到非常興奮。

洛琳：艾瑪，過來，**快一點**。

艾瑪：**別急**，我就來了，什麼東西讓妳這麼**激動**？

洛琳：妳記得我去年買的股票嗎？那家小型電腦公司的股票？

艾瑪：記得啊，它怎麼了？

洛琳：我昨天把它賣掉了，用我買時的兩倍價錢賣掉。

艾瑪：**好棒啊**！妳有多少股？

洛琳：十股。

艾瑪：十股？妳確定妳有賺到錢嗎？那佣金呢？

洛琳：誰在乎啊，妳聽我說，我剛買了另一家公司十五股的股票，我把我賺的錢又投資進去了。

艾瑪：**喔，我的天啊**。

進階解析

• What are you so + adj. + about?

意為「……讓你如此……」，如 What is she so angry about?「什麼事讓她這麼生氣？」

• commission charges

指的是美國股市的「交易佣金」，在美國股市買賣股票，每筆交易都必須給付佣金，每個股票上市公司的佣金額度不盡相同，額度較小的在十五元美金左右，額度高的會超過三十元美金，所以每筆交易光是佣金的費用就很可觀了。

• fifteen shares

十五股股票，在美國買賣股票是以每單股為一個買賣單位，而台灣的最小買賣單位是一千股。

① **Step on it.**

快一點。

例 Step on it, or I'll leave you behind.

快一點,不然我要先走了。

> **Q** —— 進階查詢 ——————
>
> 用腳踩油門。開車時踩了油門,車速就會加快。所以這個片語
> 就是要對方「動作快一點」。

② **Hold your horses.**

別急;慢慢來。

例 I'll be ready in a minute. Hold your horses.

我馬上就準備好了,你別急。

③ **worked up**

興奮;激動

例 Some people get very worked up about politics.

有些人一談到政治就變得很激動。

④ **Right on.**

好棒;太好了。

例 A: I got an A on my test!

B: Right on!

A:我考試得到 A !

B:太好了!

⑤ **Oh, brother.**

喔,我的天啊;唉呀;我的媽呀。

例 Oh, brother. Why do you always think of such strange plans.

我的天啊,你怎麼盡想些怪怪的計劃?

綠字部分為替換語詞，你也可以試著加上更多適當的替換字詞。

①

Emma,	come here. get over here. come on over.

艾瑪，過來。／過來。／過來。

②

How many shares did you	have? buy? get?

你有／買／買多少股？

③

Are you sure you	made money? profited? came out ahead?

你確定你有賺到錢嗎？／有獲利嗎？／有賺錢嗎？

✎ Exercises 動手做

A 請由本單元的片語中挑選出適當者，填入下列空格。

1. A: This is our best champagne.

   B: Oh, _____. This is going to cost me a fortune.

2. A: Can't you step _____? The movie starts at 4:30.

   B: Hold _____, Jim. We've got plenty of time.

3. A: I'm almost done.

   B: _____ on!

4. A: Do you know I've been waiting an hour?

   B: Easy, don't get all _____. I have a good excuse.

B 填空。

1. A: I just got a new cat.

   B: Oh, _____. You already have three.

2. A: We're going to Disneyland on vacation.

   B: _____! It'll be so much fun.

3. The bus is coming. _____ it.

4. It's a small problem. There's no reason to get so _____.

5. Will you please hold _____? I can't move that fast.

解答、中譯請見第 224 頁

Andrew's 精選對話

MP3 09

Robin shows up for work an hour late. His supervisor is furious.

Supervisor: What's wrong with you? It's almost 10:30!

Robin: I know, I'm sorry. My alarm clock didn't go off.

Supervisor: Save the sob story. You were supposed to give a presentation to the Everlast people.

Robin: Oh my God, it's Thursday! What happened?

Supervisor: Linda tried to cover for you, but she doesn't know the details of the case like you do.

Robin: So what happened?

Supervisor: The clients rejected our proposal. And it's all on your shoulders. You dropped the ball, Robin.

Robin: Let me call them. I may be able to patch things up.

Supervisor: You'd better, because if you don't, you're fired.

翻譯

羅賓晚了一個小時才出現在工作崗位，他的主管正在盛怒當中。

主管：你怎麼搞的？快要十點半了！

羅賓：我知道，我很抱歉，我的鬧鐘沒響。

主管：**省省吧，我一點也不同情你。**你本來應該要向永續的人做簡報的。

羅賓：喔！我的天啊，今天是星期四！結果怎樣了？

主管：琳達試著**替你做你該做的事**，不過她沒有你那麼清楚這個案子的細節。

羅賓：那後來怎樣了？

主管：客戶否決了我們的提案，而那都是**你的責任**，你**捅了大漏子了**，羅賓。

羅賓：讓我打電話給他們，或許可以**彌補我的過失**。

主管：你最好可以，因為要是你不行，你就要被炒魷魚了。

📌 進階解析

• didn't go off
鬧鐘「沒響」之意。

• the Everlast people
「the + 某團體名稱 + people」就是指「某團體的人」，如 the Taiwan University people「那些台大的人」、the MRT people「捷運公司的人」。

• You'd better
用以警告對方最好辦妥某事，如 You'd better hand in the script in three days, or you'll be in trouble.「你最好在三天內交出文稿，不然你就有麻煩了。」

⊕ 核心片語 　🎧 MP3 10

① **Save the sob story.**
省省那會讓人覺得難過的故事。

例 A: First I got in an argument with my boss. Then I lost my wallet.
B: Save the sob story. Everybody has hard days.

A：我先是跟我老闆吵了一架，然後錢包又掉了。
B：省省這些讓人難過的事吧，每個人都會有不好過的時候。

> **Q** 進階查詢
>
> sob story 指的是「會讓人難過流淚的故事」，整句之意是「叫對方省省那種賺人熱淚的故事」，亦即「別試著要我同情你的遭遇」。

② **cover for someone**
為某人代班；幫某人做其該做的事

例 I'll cover for you while you're in Europe.
你在歐洲時，我會幫你代班的。

36

③ on one's shoulders
某人要負起全部的責任

例 I know the success or failure of this assignment is on my shoulders. I won't fail.

我知道這個任務的成敗在我，我不會失敗的。

④ drop the ball
犯了一個致命的過錯

例 Come on, guys, let's get it perfect. We're almost done, so we don't want to drop the ball now.

來吧，夥伴們，把這事做得盡善盡美吧。就快完成了，所以我們不想現在把事情搞砸吧。

⑤ patch things up
修補一個很糟糕的狀況

例 Do you want me to help patch things up between you and Jasper?

你要我幫忙你跟傑斯伯和好嗎？

綠字部分為替換語詞，你也可以試著加上更多適當的替換字詞。

①

What's	wrong the matter the problem	with you?

你怎麼搞的？／怎麼回事？／有什麼問題啊？

②

My alarm clock	didn't go off. is broken. needs new batteries.

我的鬧鐘沒響。／壞了。／該換電池了。

③

The clients	rejected said they'd think over didn't like	our proposal.

客戶否決了／說他們會考慮／不喜歡我們的提案。

✎ Exercises 動手做

A 請由本單元的片語中挑選出適當者，填入下列空格。

1. A: The success or failure of this case is completely on _____.

   B: Right, so we can't afford to drop _____.

2. A: Save _____. We're almost there.

   B: But I'm tired. I've been walking all day.

3. A: It's his fault.

   B: I'm not going to be the one to _____ up this time.

4. A: Are you sure you can _____ me tomorrow?

   B: No problem.

B 填空。

1. A: So it's all up to me?

   B: I'm afraid so. It's all on _____.

2. We had a big argument. I doubt it will be easy to _____ up.

3. I don't want to hear about your problems again, so you can save _____.

4. We can let you take a couple of days off, but you'll need to find someone who can _____ you.

5. I promise I won't _____ ball again. This time I'll do a good job.

解答、中譯請見第 225 頁

為什麼要學習片語？

☑ 學習片語能大幅增加英文理解力

　　在最近的調查研究中，強調學習片語是學好英文的一個重要元素。學習者常把學習語言的重心擺在學好單一的單字上，像是 illustrate、examine 等等。雖然這是必要的，但這樣的學習方式是不足的。如果我們把每個英文單字都看成一個獨立的個體，我們很可能遺漏了許多不是單獨出現、而是由成群的字所構成的字串或片語。如果學習者習慣逐字地聽對方所說的話，這樣會嚴重地妨害學習者聽懂說話者在說什麼。所以，學習者應該要養成習慣，把注意力放在短如二個字、或長及十個字的片語上。

　　片語可分為幾種：成語、措辭、片語動詞等。片語可能是一個句子的一部份，甚至是整個句子。不幸地，每個人對片語的分類方式可能不同，所以哪個片語該歸於哪個種類有時會讓人困惑。然而，知道片語的種類並不是最重要的事。換句話說，身為學習者的你並不須太在意片語的種類，但你要學會它們的意思。這也是這本書的重點。

　　到目前為止，學習片語像是一件麻煩的任務。沒錯，學片語的確比學單字困難，但相對地，學習片語的收穫卻是比學習單字有價值。一旦學會大部分的常見片語後，你會發現你對英文的理解力增加了──不論是口說或是書寫英文。這是因為一旦你可以找出句子中的片語，句子對你而言僅是由兩到三個片語加上幾個單字所組成。把句子看成三到四個組成單位，遠比將句子看成十到十五個各別單字來得簡單。

我們來看一個簡單的例子吧：

By and large, Mike's speeches are full of hot air.
大致說來，麥克的言論都是在吹牛！

　　第一次看這個句子，它像是由十個字所組成的字串。如果你不熟悉這句子中所包含的片語，你可能會翻查字典找出所有字的意思，但卻發現你被這些字的意思搞得更糊塗了，因為這些單獨的字義並不能和前後文連結。然而，如果你對這些英文片語相當熟悉，你可立即看出這個句子包含兩個片語：by and large 和 full of hot air。所以，你應該以一組字為單位來了解其意義，而非以個別的單字為單位。（切記：片語的意義來自於組成片語的整個字串，而非個別的單字。）

　　所以，上列的例句應該是兩個片語加上三個單獨的字所構成的。這樣的確讓學習者學得更輕鬆了，不是嗎？如果你懂得 by and large 和 full of hot air 這兩個片語，其他你所須知道的就是剩下三個字的意思了「麥克的言論是……。」

☑ 了解片語才能順暢溝通

　　問題是片語需要學到什麼程度才夠好呢？一般而言，第一步是建立對常見片語的理解力，也就是能聽懂別人所說的片語。這能提昇你的聽力。聽懂了別人的意思，也就不用一直請對方再說明；同樣地，聽懂別人的意思，就可以避免誤會。下面的例子是可能會發生的情況：

Patty:　Please, eat whatever you want. Don't stand on ceremony.

Mei-lin:　Sorry, is there a special ceremony?

Patty:　I mean make yourself at home. Mi casa su casa.

Mei-lin:　Me casa what?

Patty:　Make yourself at home.

Mei-lin:　Make myself ...?

佩蒂：想吃什麼就吃什麼，請不要客氣！

美玲：抱歉，難道這裡有什麼特別的儀式嗎？

佩蒂：我的意思是把這裡當作自己家。我家就是你家啦！

美玲：我……什麼？

佩蒂：把這裡當作自己的家啦！

美玲：讓我自己怎樣？

在這個範例中我們看到佩蒂使用了三個常見的片語 Don't stand on ceremony.「不要客氣」、Mi casa su casa.「把這裡當作自己的家」、Make yourself at home.「把這裡當作自己的家」。美玲不懂得這些片語，所以誤解了佩蒂的意思，以為那裡有一個特別的儀式，然後她又不能完全理解佩蒂所說第二個片語（Mi casa su casa.）的意思，這個片語是個禮貌的用語，希望客人能舒適地在家中作客。

如果美玲知道這些片語的意思，她就能立即了解佩蒂的意思了。當某人在朋友家中作客，朋友會盡力讓客人感到舒適。上述範例中佩蒂所使用的片語就是為了達到這個目的。

再看另外一個例子：

Denny: Max dropped the ball again. I'm going to have a hard time sorting out the mess.

Mei-lin: Why was he carrying a ball?

Denny: Carrying a ball? No, you misunderstood me. I mean he's digging his own grave with the mistakes he's making.

Mei-lin: Digging his grave? Is he that sick?

Denny: No, he's not sick. He's just not doing a good job. That's all I'm trying to say.

丹尼：馬克斯又搞砸了一次。收拾這個殘局又要讓我頭大了。
美玲：為什麼他要帶顆球？
丹尼：帶顆球？不，我的意思是他正在為他所犯的錯自掘墳墓。
美玲：挖他的墳墓？他病得很嚴重嗎？
丹尼：不，他沒有生病。他只是沒有做好他的工作。這就是我想說的。

在這個例子當中，因為美玲一開始不懂丹尼所說的話，所以她並不知道馬克斯出了什麼問題。美玲只好再請丹尼說明，這也是當我們不懂對方的意思時常採用的策略。但這樣的方式也會嚴重影響對話的進行。當丹尼在解釋 drop the ball 這個片語時，他必須暫且擱置原本要進行的談話內容。此外，因為美玲也無法理解丹尼所使用的第二個片語，dig his own grave，丹尼必須再次解釋。最後，他也因為花了許多時間在解釋片語而感到精疲力盡了。

英文為母語者通常不知道如何調整他們的用語，好讓非母語者容易懂得他們的意思。畢竟英文為母語者大半輩子的時間都在使用這些用語，所以，當他們以英語和他人交談時，自然地會說出這些

用語。而且，他們通常也不知該如何解釋這些用語中的難字和難詞。

在上一個例子中，丹尼不知如何解釋 drop the ball，反而用了一個更艱深的片語 dig his own grave 來說明。這樣一來，反而使得美玲更加困惑了。

我們不能責怪丹尼。畢竟他不是一位英文老師。他根本不知道他使用了二個被非母語者歸類為成語的片語。再者，他也不習慣解釋這類片語。他習慣用很快的速度說英文，並穿插使用片語。所以，當他必須解釋他所說的話時，他以往的溝通模式就被打破，訊息的交流也暫時中斷。

我們可以看出了解片語意思的重要性——也就是懂得別人在說些什麼。扮演一個好的聽眾和成為一個好的說話者一樣重要。在口語的聽力上有紮實的基礎可以提昇一個人全面的英文能力，可以避免困窘的情況，也可以確保溝通進行得很順暢。

Chapter 2

The Workplace 工作場合

英語學習專欄② 該學哪些片語呢？

Andrew's 精選對話

MP3 11

Laureen gets a phone call from her colleague Catherine.

Laureen: Hey, Catherine, how goes it?

Catherine: Same old, same old. I haven't seen you at the office for a while.

Laureen: I've been doing most of my work at home.

Catherine: At home? How do you get away with that?

Laureen: I do my work on my PC. Then, I e-mail the files to my supervisor.

Catherine: Don't you need to talk with anyone at the office?

Laureen: I can do that on the phone. Still, I go by the office about once a week.

Catherine: You lucky dog. It sounds like you've got it made.

Laureen: I can't complain. Life's pretty good right now.

翻譯

蘿琳接到一通她同事凱瑟琳打來的電話。

蘿琳　　：嗨，凱瑟琳，**妳好嗎**？
凱瑟琳：**還是老樣子**，我有好一陣子沒在辦公室見到妳。
蘿琳　　：我一直是在家裡處理大部分的工作。
凱瑟琳：在家**妳怎麼辦到的**？
蘿琳　　：我用我的個人電腦做事，然後把檔案用電子郵件寄給我的主管。
凱瑟琳：妳難道不須跟辦公室裡的人溝通嗎？
蘿琳　　：我可以用電話解決。不過我大概還是會每個禮拜到辦公室一趟。
凱瑟琳：**妳真的非常幸運，聽起來妳往後的生活會過得很好。**
蘿琳　　：還不錯啦，現在的生活確實是蠻好的。

🔖 進階解析

- **I haven't seen you at the office for a while.**

當某人／事／物已經不做某動作或不處於某種狀態一段時間了，可以用「S + have/has not + p.p. + for a while」這個說法。

- **PC**

即為 personal computer「個人電腦」。

- **e-mail**

「電子郵件」這個字，既是名詞也是動詞，當名詞時，就是寄 e-mail 給某人，當動詞時，則是把一些檔案 e-mail 給某人。

- **Life's pretty good.**

即 My life's pretty good.。

① **How goes it?**

你好嗎？

例 A: Hello!

　　B: Hi, Bob. How goes it?

　　A：哈囉！

　　B：嗨，巴布，你好嗎？

② **Same old, same old.**

還是老樣子。

例 A: What are you up to these days?

　　B: Same old, same old.

　　A：你近來如何？

　　B：還是老樣子。

> **Q** 　進階查詢
>
> 就是 I've been doing the same old thing.「我一直都在做著相同的事」，也就是中文的「老樣子」了。

③ **get away with something**
辦成某事

例 How did you get away with buying that so cheaply?
你怎麼有辦法用那麼便宜的價格買到那個？

④ **You lucky dog.**
你真的非常幸運。

例 A: Susan wants to go with me to the dance!
B: You lucky dog.
A：蘇珊想跟我去舞會！
B：你真是幸運。

⑤ **You've got it made.**
你現在的基礎打好了，以後一定過得不錯。

例 A: My new company is giving me stock options.
B: You've got it made. You'll be rich before you're thirty.
A：我的新公司給我配股。
B：你的後路有著落了，三十歲以前就能致富。

綠字部分為替換語詞，你也可以試著加上更多適當的替換字詞。

①

I haven't seen you	at the office at work around	for a while.

我有好一陣子沒在辦公室／在公司／在這兒見到你。

②

I can do that	on the phone. by phone. over the telephone.

我可以在電話上／用電話／透過電話解決。

③

Still, I	go by stop by check in at	the office about once a week.

不過我大概還是會每個禮拜到辦公室去一趟。／去一趟。／報告一下進度。

✏ Exercises 動手做

A 請由本單元的片語中挑選出適當者，填入下列空格。

1. You should have known you'd never get _____ it.

2. _____ dog. With all the money you made from the stock market, you've got _____.

3. A: It's good to see you. How _____ it?
   B: Same _____. How about yourself?

B 選擇正確的字。

1. After winning all that money, you've got/won it made.

2. A: How's everything?
   B: Same old/way, same old/way.

3. I don't think you're going to get away for/with that.

4. You lucky dog/cat. I never win anything, and you just won a new car!

5. A: How goes you/it, Trish?
   B: Hey, Flo. I'm pretty good. How about you?

解答、中譯請見第 226 頁

Andrew's 精選對話

🎧 MP3 13

Sally owns a hair salon. Her friend Doris stops by to visit.

Doris: So, how's business been?

Sally: We're getting by all right. The weekends have been very good.

Doris: Great. How's that new hairdresser doing?

Sally: Not bad. I wasn't sure about her at first, but the customers seem to like her.

Doris: Fancy that.

Sally: Yeah. Now I'm hoping the landlord doesn't raise the rent. Our lease is up next month.

Doris: I'll keep my fingers crossed for you. Running a small business isn't easy, is it?

Sally: Not by a long shot.

Doris: It looks like a few customers are coming in. I'll get out of your hair.

Sally: All right. See you later, Doris. Thanks for coming by.

翻譯

莎莉擁有一家美髮店，她朋友朵莉絲順道經過來看看她。

朵莉絲：生意如何？

莎莉　：我們**做得**不錯，週末生意都很好。

朵莉絲：太棒了，新來的美髮師做得如何？

莎莉　：還不錯，一開始我對她沒什麼把握，不過客人好像都蠻喜歡她的。

朵莉絲：**那就太好了。**

莎莉　：是啊，現在我則是希望房東不要漲房租，我們的租約下個月到期。

朵莉絲：**我會替妳祈禱的**，經營個小生意不容易，對吧？

莎莉　：**絕對不是件易事。**

朵莉絲：看來有幾個客人要進來了，我就**不打擾妳了**。

莎莉　：好啊，回頭見，朵莉絲，謝謝妳來看我。

📌 進階解析

● not sure about + N/Ving

「對……不確定」，如 Joan is not sure about going to night school after work.
「瓊不是很確定下班後是否要去夜校進修。」

● lease is up

意為「租約到期」。

● running a small business

「經營一個小生意」，「經營」這個詞的英文為「run」。

① **get by**

活得下去；過得去；撐過某個狀況

例 Now that Father has lost his job, I don't know how we'll get by.

現在老爸丟了工作，我不知道我們該怎麼撐下去。

---

② **Fancy that.**

那就太令人驚訝了；太有趣了；太好了。

例 A: These wool sweaters are on sale.

B: Fancy that. Last week they were still full price.

A：這些羊毛衣正在特價拍賣。

B：太好了，上個禮拜它們還以原價出售呢。

---

③ **keep one's fingers crossed**

祈禱好運

例 A: There's a chance the Lakers may lose this basketball game.

B: Keep your fingers crossed and hope they don't!

A：湖人隊有可能輸了這場籃球賽的。

B：你還是祈禱希望他們不會輸吧！

④ **Not by a long shot.**

絕對不可能；連「接近」都談不上。

例 The construction isn't nearly completed. Not by a long shot.

這個建築物並沒有接近完工，連「幾乎」都談不上。

⑤ **get out of someone's hair**

不再與某人說話；不再打擾某人

例 Run along and get out of your mother's hair. She's very busy.

走開，別再打擾你媽媽，她很忙的。

> **Q** 進階查詢
>
> 某物在某人的頭髮裡，會使某人厭煩，如果把東西揪出來，就不會再使某人厭煩，因此這個片語就是「不再煩某人」的意思。

綠字部分為替換語詞，你也可以試著加上更多適當的替換字詞。

①

We're getting by	all right. well enough. as best we can.

我們過得不錯。／夠好了。／儘可能地好。

②

Our lease	is up expires needs to be renewed	next month.

我們的租約下個月到期。／到期。／得更新。

③

Running a small business Being your own boss Supervising a lot of employees	isn't easy, is it?

經營個小生意／自己當老闆／管理很多員工不容易，對吧？

✏ **Exercises** 動手做

A 請由本單元的片語中挑選出適當者，填入下列空格。

1. A: I know you're busy, so I'll get _____.
   B: That's all right. It's always a pleasure to talk with you.

2. A: You're not even as fast as me. Not by _____.
   B: I know. Slow down!

3. _____ that. I got all my work done, and it's only 2:30.

4. A: If I don't get that job, I'm not sure how I'll _____ by.
   B: I'll keep _____ for you.

5. A: Arlene says she wants to be an accountant.
   B: _____. I thought she didn't like math.

6. A: I should get _____.
   B: Nonsense. I'm enjoying the company.

7. People say the hotel industry isn't doing well. Are you _____ all right?

8. The game is not over yet. Not by _____.

9. They're about to draw the winning ticket. Keep _____.

解答、中譯請見第 226 頁

Andrew's 精選對話

MP3 15

Vinny and Theodore are colleagues. Their work spaces are next to each other.

Vinny: How are you doing over there?

Theodore: Not much to say, but I could kill for some coffee.

Vinny: Listen, Theodore, I don't want to come off as rude, but there's something I need to get off my chest.

Theodore: Let's have it.

Vinny: It's about your radio. I've been having trouble concentrating.

Theodore: I'll turn it off.

Vinny: No, you don't have to do that. Just a bit lower would be fine.

Theodore: Sure thing. What do you say we take a breather? I'll buy you a cup of coffee.

Vinny: Thanks. That would be great.

翻譯

文尼和瑟厄多是同事，他們的工作空間相鄰接。

文尼　　：你在那邊還好嗎？

瑟厄多：沒什麼可說的，不過我**真的很想喝些咖啡**。

文尼　　：聽著，瑟厄多，我不想**表現得**很無禮，不過有件事我一定得**一吐為快**。

瑟厄多：**你說啊**。

文尼　　：跟你的收音機有關，我一直沒辦法專心。

瑟厄多：那我會把它關掉。

文尼　　：那倒不必，只要把聲音調小就好了。

瑟厄多：當然沒問題，我們**休息一會兒**如何？我請你喝杯咖啡。

文尼　　：謝謝，那太棒了。

進階解析

• Not much to say.

即 There's not much to say. ，將 There's 省略了。

• I could kill for + N

字面意思是「我可以為了⋯⋯而殺人」，引自為「我非常想要⋯⋯」。

• I'll buy you + N

「我會買⋯⋯給你」的意思，即為「我請你⋯⋯」，如 I'll buy you a drink. 「我請你喝飲料。」

① **I could kill for something.**

我真的很想要某個東西。

例 I could kill for a hot dog right now.

我現在真想吃一條熱狗。

---

② **come off as**

表現得……；給人……的感覺

例 He comes off as being shy, but he really isn't.

他表現得很害羞，其實他一點也不害羞。

---

③ **get something off one's chest**

一吐為快；大聲表示出來

例 I'm glad I got that off my chest. I've been meaning to tell you for a long time.

我很高興能一吐為快，我一直都想告訴你的。

---

④ **Let's have it.**

告訴我;說來聽聽。

例 A: I've got the final score here.

B: Let's have it.

A:我的最後成績出來了。

B:說來聽聽啊。

⑤ **take a breather**

稍微休息一下;短時間暫停一下

例 I'm going to take a breather and have a seat under those trees.

我要到那些樹下找個位子稍微休息一下。

Q 進階查詢

「停下來喘口氣」的意思,就如爬山很累時,要先停下來喘口氣,然後再往上走,所以這個動作就有「停下來休息一下」的意思。

☑ 精挑句型

綠字部分為替換語詞，你也可以試著加上更多適當的替換字詞。

①

How are you doing How's everything going What's going on	over there?

你那邊的工作／你那邊的事情／事情進行得怎麼樣了？

②

I've been having trouble	concentrating. getting my work done. doing my job.

我一直沒辦法專注。／做完我的工作。／做事。

③

No,	you don't have you don't need there's no need	to do that.

不用，那倒不必。／那倒不需要。／沒那必要。

✏ **Exercises** 動手做

A 請由本單元的片語中挑選出適當者，填入下列空格。

1. A: I've wanted to say that for a long time. I'm glad I
   _____ chest.
   B: You know, you _____ as a tough guy, but you're
   actually sensitive.
2. A: I'm hungry.
   B: Me too. I _____ for some Mexican food.
3. A: Do you want to take _____ in a few minutes?
   B: Good idea.
4. A: I just thought of a great idea.
   B: Let's _____.

B 填空。

1. A: I've got some wonderful news!
   B: Let's have _____.
2. I need to get this off my _____, so please listen.
3. A: I'm so hungry.
   B: Me too. I could _____ for a pizza.
4. We don't have the time to _____ a breather.
5. The way she dresses and speaks, Katie comes off
   _____ very conservative.

解答、中譯請見第 227 頁

Andrew's 精選對話

MP3 17

Lilian's car is in the shop. Her colleague gives her a ride home.

Lilian: We're almost at my house.

Stuart: You live in a beautiful neighborhood.

Lilian: Why, thank you. Slow down a bit ... OK, this is me.

Stuart: Right here?

Lilian: Yes, that's perfect. Do you want to come in for a drink?

Stuart: No, I need to get home.

Lilian: Well, thanks for the ride. Sorry to put you out like that. I owe you one.

Stuart: Don't worry about it. I've had my share of car troubles before, so I can relate. Do you need a ride to work tomorrow?

Lilian: No, no, but you are so kind to ask. My mechanic said I can pick my car up in the morning.

Stuart: Then I'll see you at work tomorrow.

翻譯

莉莉安的車子在修理廠裡，她的同事載她回家。

莉莉安　　：我們幾乎到我家了。

斯圖亞特：妳住的鄰近地區很漂亮。

莉莉安　　：喔，謝謝你。慢一點……好了，**這裡就是我家**。

斯圖亞特：就在這兒嗎？

莉莉安　　：對啊，剛好就在門口，你要進來喝點什麼嗎？

斯圖亞特：不了，我要回去了。

莉莉安　　：謝謝你載我回來，**很抱歉**要那麼**麻煩你，我欠你個人情**。

斯圖亞特：別在意，**我以前也有過車子的問題**，所以**我能體會妳的情形**。明
　　　　　天需要我載妳去上班嗎？

莉莉安　　：不，不用了，不過你會這樣問真好心，我的維修師傅說我明天早
　　　　　上可以去取車。

斯圖亞特：那麼，明天公司見了。

進階解析

• **Why, thank you.**
Why 不是「為什麼」的意思，why 在此沒有任何意義，只是表示 Oh「喔」
的語助詞。

• **I need to get home.**
當然也可以說 I need to go home.，口語中「回家」常用 get home 來表示。

① **This is me.**

這裡就是我住的地方。

例 This is me. Thanks for the ride.

　　這裡就是我住的地方,謝謝你載我回來。

> 🔍 ── 進階查詢
>
> 原來是說 This is where I live. 或 This is my house.,因為 where I live 和 my house 都是指「我住的地方」,所以就簡化成 This is me.,用 me 來代表「我的住處」。

② **Sorry to put you out.**

很抱歉增添你的麻煩;很抱歉麻煩你。

例 A: Sorry to put you out.

　　B: It was no trouble at all.

　　A:很抱歉增添了你的麻煩。

　　B:一點也不麻煩。

③ **I owe you one.**

我欠你一個人情。

例 I couldn't have succeeded without you. I owe you one.

沒有你我不可能成功的，我欠你個人情。

④ **I've had my share of N**

我也有過很多⋯⋯的麻煩。

例 I've had my share of bad luck this week.

我這個禮拜的運氣也很差啊。

⑤ **I can relate.**

我能體會你的感受，我能體會你的狀況。

例 A: I'm so tired, I can barely move.

B: I can relate. I felt the same way after work yesterday.

A：我好累，我幾乎沒力氣動了。

B：我可以體會，我昨天下班後也有同樣的感覺。

☑ 精挑句型

綠字部分為替換語詞，你也可以試著加上更多適當的替換字詞。

①

We're	almost at just about at getting near	my house.

我們幾乎快到／快到／正在接近我家了。

②

Do you want to	come in for a drink? have something to eat? take a snack with you?

你要進來喝點什麼嗎？／吃點東西嗎？／帶些零食嗎？

③

Do you need	a ride a lift me to take you	to work tomorrow?

明天需要我來載你／我來載你／我來載你去上班嗎？

✏ Exercises 動手做

A 請由本單元的片語中挑選出適當者，填入下列空格。

1. A: Thanks for the help setting up the generator, neighbor. Sorry _____ out.

   B: Any time! I've also had _____ electrical problems.

2. A: Well, this _____. Thanks again.

   B: You're welcome. I've asked lots of people for rides before, so _____ relate.

3. A: I appreciate your helping me study for the chemistry test. I _____ one.

   B: I'm glad I could help.

4. I am so grateful you let me borrow your car. I _____.

5. A: There are so many weeds in my garden!

   B: Maybe I can help. I've had _____ problems with weeds.

6. A: If I give you a ride, I'll miss the basketball game on TV.

   B: I am so sorry to _____, but you're my last hope.

7. A: Do you know what I mean?

   B: I sure do. I've had similar experiences, so I _____.

8. This _____. You can let me off at the corner.

解答、中譯請見第 228 頁

Andrew's 精選對話

🎧 MP3 19

Jeff and Melissa work at the same company, but in different departments.

Jeff: Things have changed for the worse in our department since you transferred out.

Melissa: Really? I've been out of the loop for a while. I had no idea things were so bad.

Jeff: I'll fill you in. Did you know Brenda Hammerson left?

Melissa: No, I didn't.

Jeff: Her replacement is a total dictator. He made all these new rules — about what we can wear, how long our breaks can be, how many sick days we can take …

Melissa: Not good.

Jeff: Then he posted the rules on the bulletin board, so they'd always be there in black and white.

Melissa: No way! I feel for you, Jeff. But I'm glad I don't have to deal with that guy!

翻譯

傑夫和美黎莎在同一家公司的不同部門做事。

傑夫　：自從妳轉到別的部門後，我們部門的**狀況變糟了**。

美黎莎：真的嗎？我已經**不在那兒**好一陣子了，我一點也不知道事情有這麼糟。

傑夫　：我**慢慢告訴妳**吧，妳知道布蘭達‧漢莫森離開了嗎？

美黎莎：我不知道。

傑夫　：接替她的人是個完全的獨裁者，他訂的新規定包括：限定我們該穿什麼、休息時間有多長、病假能請幾天……

美黎莎：不太妙啊。

傑夫　：然後他還把這些規定貼到佈告欄上，所以它們就是**白紙黑字**一直得遵守的了。

美黎莎：不可能！**我替你感到難過**，傑夫，不過，我很慶幸我不必跟那傢伙打交道。

✎ **進階解析**

● **I had no idea.**

即為 I didn't know.「我不知道。」的意思。

● **sick days**

即為「病假」，在英文中，請假的種類沒有事假、公假、病假、產假……等這麼多類別，而只有兩種 sick days「病假」與 vacation days「假期」。

● **deal with + N**

deal with 其後接某人，意思為「與某人周旋，與某人打交道」，若接某事，意思則為「處理某事」。

① **for the worse**
使情況更糟

例 These changes to the dress code are for the worse.
服裝規範的改變使得情況變得更糟了。

② **out of the loop**
不再是某個團體或情況的一部分

例 Since my father retired, he's been out of the loop with his former company.
自從我父親退休後，他就不再是他之前公司的一分子了。

③ **fill someone in**
慢慢地、詳細地告訴某人

例 Let me fill you in on what happened here while you were on your business trip.
我來慢慢告訴你在你出差時這裡發生了什麼事。

> **Q 進階查詢**
>
> 對某人做出「填入」的動作，當某人對某事一無所知，就像支沒裝滿的瓶子，而告訴他所有的詳細情形，就像是填滿這支瓶子似的，因此這動作就用來表示「詳細告訴某人」之意。

④ **in black and white**

白紙黑字寫得清清楚楚的

例 The terms of our agreement are right here in black and white.

我們的同意協定在這兒——白紙黑字寫得很清楚。

⑤ **I feel for you.**

我能體會你的感受；我替你感到難過。

例 A: I've been studying for this test every day and night for three months.

B: I feel for you. It must be very hard.

A：我為了這個考試不眠不休地讀了三個月。

B：我能體會你的感受，一定非常辛苦。

☑ 精挑句型

綠字部分為替換語詞，你也可以試著加上更多適當的替換字詞。

①

I had no idea things	were so bad.
	had gotten so bad.
	had worsened so much.

我一點也不知道事情有這麼糟。／變得這麼糟。／糟糕到這種地步。

②

Her replacement is	a total dictator.
	hard to get along with.
	fond of giving everybody orders.

接替她的人是個完全的獨裁者。／難以相處的人。／喜歡命令別人的人。

③

I feel	for you.
	bad for you.
	sorry for you.

我為你感到難過。／為你感到難過。／為你感到難過。

✎ **Exercises** 動手做

A 請由本單元的片語中挑選出適當者，填入下列空格。

1. You don't know Hakeem got married? You really are out _____.

2. We both agreed to it in the contract. It's written there, in _____.

3. Events have changed _____ worse now that the fire has spread out of control.

4. A: I hope you guys can fill _____ about the class when I get back next week. I'm worried I'll fall behind.
   B: I feel _____. It's hard to catch up after a week.
   C: Too true!

B 選擇正確的字。

1. The code is written out clearly, in black then/and white.

2. His new friends have affected him for/to the worse.

3. I still need you to tell/fill me in about the meeting.

4. I really do feel for you/sorry, but I don't see how I can help.

5. You have no idea what's going on because you've been out of the circle/loop.

解答、中譯請見第 228 頁

該學哪些片語呢？

正如先前所提到的，片語可分為成語、措辭和片語動詞。書中大部分的片語屬於前兩種，因為它們較難而且需要較多的說明，而片語動詞通常只有兩個字（動詞＋介系詞），很容易在字典中查到。

☑ 不同情境的片語

片語是生活中很重要的一部分，所以我們必須學會並能夠在不同場合中使用。本書依照情境主題分為 7 章，告訴你這些常見的片語在不同的情境下該如何使用、並如何回應。以「A Business Plan 創業計畫」這個單元為例，珍妮和派翠西亞二人在討論一個新的生意，珍妮想要得到派翠西亞的注意，所以她用了 get this「聽聽這個」這個片語。而在下一句中，派翠西亞想要確認珍妮說了什麼，於是用了 come again「再說一次」這個片語。這段對話中的其他片語也幫助了她們二人的討論。

☑ 不同功能的片語

你也須學習具有不同功能的片語（例如「問候」或是「道再見」），以「The End of a Visit 拜訪末了」這個單元為例，我們看到班與克里斯二人在道別，班想表達要離開的意願，於是說了 get on his horse 這個片語，意思是「要走了」。班想讓克里斯知道他會保持聯繫，於是說了 I'll give you a buzz.「我會打電話給你」。

這本書介紹了許多片語，這些片語可以用在不同的情境，也包含了許多不同的功能。如果你能全部學會，你就能應付諸多不同的

情況。這些片語將會協助你與英文為母語者的溝通。

　　如果你希望你的英文顯得靈活而有變化，我會建議你在日常的談話中使用一些片語。當然，這意謂著你必須決定要使用哪些詞語。我建議你多聽聽外國朋友或是同事所使用的片語。藉著使用一些他們的用語，可以增加你在那個團體中的被認同感。或許，你有特別偏愛的片語，試著去使用它，如果得到的反應是正面的，就繼續使用，為你的英文添加一些個人的特質。

Chapter 3

Money & Shopping 金錢與購物

- **Day 11** The Parking Ticket
- **Day 12** I Have to Have it!
- **Day 13** Buying a New Computer

英語學習專欄 ③ 使用片語的時機

The Parking Ticket

違規停車罰單

Andrew's 精選對話

(🎧) MP3 21

John's car is illegally parked on a busy street. He sees a police officer writing him a ticket.

John: Is that ticket for me?

Officer: If that's your car, then yes.

John: But I was about to leave. Come on, cut me some slack.

Officer: Sorry, I can't do that.

John: Just rip up the ticket. I won't tell a soul. I promise.

Officer: Sir, I think you're missing the point. You broke the law, and now you have to face the music.

John: All right, save the lecture and give me the ticket.

Officer: Here you are. Have a good one.

John: Gee, thanks. You too.

翻譯

約翰的車違規停在交通繁忙的街道上，他看到一個交通警察正在開他罰單。

約翰：那張罰單是給我的嗎？
警察：如果這是你的車的話，那麼是的。
約翰：不過，我正要離開，拜託，**放個水嘛**。
警察：抱歉，我不能那麼做。
約翰：只要把罰單撕掉就好，**我不會告訴別人的**，我發誓。
警察：先生，我想**你還沒明白重點吧**，你犯了法，你得**為自己所犯的錯受罰**。
約翰：好吧，別再說教了，把那張罰單給我吧。
警察：這是你的罰單，**祝你愉快**。
約翰：唉，謝啦，也祝你愉快。

🖈 進階解析

• You broke the law.

「你破壞了法規」即「你違法」之意，「犯法；違法」都可以用 break the law 來表示。

• save the lecture

「省下長篇大論」之意，這裡的 lecture 不是演講，而是指「說教」、「長篇大論」等。

• Gee, thanks.

在這裡並不是真的感謝對方，而是反過來調刺對方的說辭。

① **Cut me some slack.**

別對我這麼嚴苛。

例 Cut me some slack. I was only five minutes late.

別對我這麼嚴苛嘛,我才不過遲到五分鐘。

> Q　　**進階查詢**
>
> slack 就是布的縐摺,穿著衣褲時,肘彎處、胯部及膝蓋處若沒有縐摺,就會覺得衣褲很緊不舒服,所以 cut me some slack「多剪一些布給我當縐摺」就被引申為「別對我那麼嚴格;讓我輕鬆一點」。

② **I won't tell a soul.**

我不會告訴別人。

例 That's a pretty big secret. I promise I won't tell a soul.

那可是個天大的祕密,我答應你不會告訴任何人的。

③ **You're missing the point.**

你沒抓住重點；你不了解重點。

例 A: But we can save money this way.

B: You're missing the point. That method may save money, but it'll lower the quality too much.

A：但是，這樣我們可以省錢啊。

B：你沒抓住重點，那個方法也許可以省錢，不過卻會大幅地降低品質。

④ **face the music**

自作自受

例 When Dad gets home, we'll all have to face the music.

等爸爸一回到家，我們就得自嚐苦果了。

⑤ **Have a good one.**

祝你愉快。（註：one 指某段不確定的時間）

例 I'll talk to you later. Have a good one.

我們以後再聊吧，祝你愉快。

綠字部分為替換語詞，你也可以試著加上更多適當的替換字詞。

①

If	that's your car, you parked there, you're this car's owner,	then yes.

如果那是你的車，／你在這兒停車，／你是這輛車的主人，那麼是的。

②

But, I was	about getting ready all set	to leave.

不過，我正要／準備要／都準備好要離開。

③

Just	rip up throw away tear up	the ticket.

只要把罰單撕掉／丟掉／撕掉就好。

✎ Exercises 動手做

A 請由本單元的片語中挑選出適當者，填入下列空格。

1. A: I've got to go. See you later.
   B: Have a _____.

2. A: Careful. If you break anything, you'll have to face _____.
   B: Cut _____. I never break anything.

3. A: I know there's a mistake, but I won't tell _____ if you won't.
   B: You're missing _____. It's our responsibility to do a good job.

B 選擇正確的字。

1. Have the/a good one.

2. Can you please cut me some space/slack?

3. Like I said, I won't tell a soul/ghost.

4. Eventually, every criminal has to face/hear the music.

5. You're still missing the key/point. I'll explain what I mean again.

解答、中譯請見第 229 頁

Andrew's 精選對話　　　　　　　　　　🎧 MP3 23

It's March 6th. Allen and his wife Gina are browsing in a department store.

Allen: Ooh, look at that coffee machine!

Gina: Here we go again. Allen, we saw that same machine here last month.

Allen: I know. It's fantastic, isn't it?

Gina: I guess, but we can't afford it.

Allen: Sure we can. I just got paid yesterday. And with this machine, we'll save money.

Gina: How do you figure?

Allen: Instead of going to coffee shops, we can make coffee at home!

Gina: Hah! That's a good one.

Allen: Come on, be a sport.

Gina: All right, I give in. Let's get it.

翻譯

三月六日，艾倫和他老婆吉娜正在百貨公司裡逛著。

艾倫：喔，妳看那個煮咖啡機！

吉娜：**又來了**。艾倫，我們上個月也在這兒看過同樣的機器。

艾倫：我知道，這個機器很棒，不是嗎？

吉娜：應該是吧，我們買不起的。

艾倫：我們當然可以，我昨天剛領薪水，而且，有了這個機器，我們就可以省錢。

吉娜：**你這想法哪來的？**

艾倫：我們可以在家煮咖啡，不用去咖啡店了。

吉娜：哈！**那可真好笑**。

艾倫：別這樣嘛，跟我一起享受一下嘛。

吉娜：好吧，**我附議**，我們買吧。

進階解析

• **I guess, ...**

在這裡是「應該是」之意，語氣不是很確定，可以用在不想回答對或不對的時候。

• **With this machine, we'll save money.**

「With + N, S+V」的句型。例：With this map, we can find the place.「用這張地圖，我們可以找到地方。」

• **Instead of V₁-ing, S + V₂**

指主詞做某事（V_2）以取代另一件事（V_1），例：Instead of going to the swimming pool, we went to the beach.「我們去海邊玩，而不是去游泳池。」

① **Here we go again.**

又來了；相同的事又再發生一遍了。

例 A: The car needs some repairs.

B: Here we go again. How much will it cost this time?

A：這部車需要修一修。

B：又來了，這次要花多少錢啊？

② **How do you figure?**

你這想法哪來的；你如何得到這種結論？

例 A: This method should save us a lot of time.

B: How do you figure?

A：這個方法應該會幫我們省很多時間。

B：你這結論哪來的？

③ **That's a good one.**

真好笑；這個笑話很好笑。

例 That's a good one. Where'd you hear it?

這個笑話真好笑，你從哪裡聽來的？

> **Q 進階查詢**
>
> 即 That's a good joke. 之意，用來表示對方所說的話很好笑。

④ Be a sport.

參一腳；和其他人一起渡過美好時光。

例 Be a sport. You'll have a good time.

來參一腳吧，你會玩得很愉快的。

⑤ I give in

我附議；我同意你的計畫。

例 A: Carl, you're the only one who hasn't said yes.

B: All right, I give in. Yes.

A：卡爾，你是唯一還沒答應的人。

B：好吧，我附議，好的。

☑ 精挑句型

綠字部分為替換語詞，你也可以試著加上更多適當的替換字詞。

①

	coffee machine!
Ooh, look at that	sofa.
	set of silverware.

喔，你看那個煮咖啡機！／座沙發。／組銀器。

②

Sure	
Of course	**we can.**
Yes,	

我們當然／當然／是可以的。

③

	got paid	
I just	got my paycheck	**yesterday.**
	received my salary	

我昨天剛領薪水。／拿到薪水支票。／領薪水。

✏️ Exercises 動手做

A 請由本單元的片語中挑選出適當者，填入下列空格。

1. A: Go camping with us. It'll be fun. Be _____.
   B: It'll be fun? That's _____ one. I was sore for a week after the last time we went camping.

2. A: Come on, let's buy it?
   B: OK, I _____ in.

3. A: See, this is really a great deal.
   B: _____ figure? It doesn't look good to me.

4. A: I need you to work overtime.
   B: Here _____. This happens every week.

5. A: Follow me, everybody.
   B: Here we go _____.

6. A: But I don't like to sing.
   B: Be a _____. It'll be fun.

7. No, I won't _____ in. I refuse to participate.

8. A: We should be there in five hours.
   B: How do you _____? It usually takes at least seven hours.

9. _____ a good one. I needed a good laugh.

解答、中譯請見第 230 頁

Andrew's 精選對話

MP3 25

Adam wants to buy a new computer. He has a friend who works in a computer store.

Adam: Can you help me put together a new system?

Earl: Sure I can.

Adam: But nothing that'll put me in the poor house.

Earl: Don't you worry. I'll do you right. Now, what kind of sound card and video card do you want?

Adam: What kind of what? All that computer talk is over my head.

Earl: OK, what will you use the system for? Work, games, graphics, surfing the Internet — what?

Adam: Mostly for the Internet. My son might like to play games.

Earl: What price did you have in mind?

Adam: Maybe $1,000 or so.

Earl: No problem. I think I have something that's right up your alley.

翻譯

亞當想買台新電腦，他朋友在一家電腦店工作。

亞當：你能幫我組一台新電腦嗎？

厄爾：當然可以。

亞當：不過，不要那些**會花我很多錢**的東西。

厄爾：你別擔心，我**不會讓你吃虧的**。那麼，你想要什麼樣的音效卡跟顯示卡？

亞當：什麼什麼卡？那些電腦用語**超出我的理解範圍**。

厄爾：好吧，你要用這部電腦來做什麼？工作、玩遊戲、電腦繪圖、上網……等等，要做什麼？

亞當：大部分是上網用，我兒子可能會想玩遊戲。

厄爾：你**想花多少錢**呢？

亞當：大概一千塊錢左右吧。

厄爾：沒問題，我想我有些東西**蠻符合你的需求**。

🖈 進階解析

• put together a system

system 是指 computer system「電腦系統」，用 put together 是因為一部電腦必須由好幾個個別的組件（卡）組裝在一起才有作用，所以用這個片語來表示組電腦。

• computer talk

「電腦的用語」之意，「N + talk」指的就是「……用語」，如：business talk「商業用語」。

• surfing the Internet

「在網際網路上到處瀏覽」之意，會用 surf 這個字是因為在網路世界裡，隨意按連結到處瀏覽的樣子，就像看電視時拿著遙控器一直轉台的動作（channel surf）。

① **put someone in the poor house**
讓某人花很多錢

例 I love that stereo, but if I buy it, it'll put me in the poor house.

我好喜歡那台音響，不過我如果買了它，我會破產的。

> 🔍　進階查詢
>
> 表示某人已經散盡家財，只能住到破爛的房子裡了，所以引申有「讓某人花了很多錢」的意思。

② **do someone right**
公平對待某人；不讓某人吃虧

例 You can rely on Thomas. He'll do you right.

你可以倚賴湯瑪士，他不會讓你吃虧的。

③ **over my head**
對我來說太艱深複雜而難懂

例 Most of his ideas are over my head.
他大部分的點子都超出我的理解範圍。

④ **have in mind**
想；考慮

例 If $100 is too much, what price did you have in mind?
如果一百塊太貴，你想花多少錢呢？

⑤ **right up your alley**
蠻適合你的

例 I recently read a book that may be right up your alley.
我最近看了本書，那本書蠻適合你的。

☑ 精挑句型

綠字部分為替換語詞，你也可以試著加上更多適當的替換字詞。

①

Can you help me	put together a new system?
	fix my computer?
	find out what's wrong with my computer?

你能幫我組一台新電腦嗎？／修理我的電腦嗎？／看看我的電腦出了什麼問題嗎？

②

All that	computer talk	is over my head.
	technical info	
	talk about programming	

那些電腦用語／技術資訊／有關程式的談話超出我的理解範圍。

③

My son might like to	play games.
	surf the Internet.
	use some graphics programs.

我兒子可能會想玩遊戲。／上網。／用某些繪圖軟體。

✏ **Exercises** 動手做

A 請由本單元的片語中挑選出適當者，填入下列空格。

1. A: What kind of new car did you _____ mind?
   B: A nice one, as long as it doesn't _____.

2. A: Everything the professor said today was over _____.
   B: Me too.

3. You can trust me about this car. Like I said, I'll do
   _____.

4. A: This project might be right _____.
   B: It is in my field of expertise.

5. You can trust me. I'll do you _____.

6. A picnic sounds like fun. Where did you have in _____?

7. Do you understand what she's saying? It's all _____
   my head.

8. All right, I'll give you a discount. I don't want to put you in
   the _____ house.

9. There's a television program on about birds. That's right up
   your _____.

解答、中譯請見第 231 頁

使用片語的時機

☑ 大部分的片語都可以安心的廣泛使用

一般而言，大部分的片語都可以安全地使用在大多數的場合。成語（一種固定的措辭）和其他種類的片語幾乎都可用在所有的談話場合中。片語不像其他種類的口語英文（像是俚語），你不須擔心使用時可能會冒犯別人。

☑ 片語要正確完整的使用原貌，而不要隨意換字

然而，你在使用片語時有兩個須要注意的地方。第一，你使用的片語必須完全是你原先學到的樣子：該包含的字不能漏掉以及字的順序不能改變。漏了一個字可能會改變片語的意思、妨礙了對話的進行，聽者可能會感到困惑，甚至誤解了你的意思。

下列有二個例子。第一個例子中的錯誤是無意的，但由於一個字的錯誤，對話的進行就因而中斷了。

• 錯漏字造成對方困惑的例子

Jack: That was a tough negotiation.

Mr. Lin: It sure was. Those guys have a no holding barred way of negotiating.

Jack: They have a what?

Mr. Lin: No holding barred. Is that right?

Jack: Oh, you mean "no-holds-barred."

Mr. Lin: That's right.

傑克　　：這個協商真是棘手啊。
林先生：的確是。這些傢伙協商的方式真是「不擇手段」。
傑克　　：他們有什麼？
林先生：「不擇手段」啊，不是嗎？
傑克　　：喔，你的意思是「不擇手段」。
林先生：嗯，沒錯。

　　第二個例子的錯誤較為嚴重，由於片語的使用不正確而造成了誤解。

• 隨意改變片語，而造成誤解的例子

Kate:　　　It's so hot!

Zhou-wei:　I know. I could kill you for an ice cream.

Kate:　　　Kill me? Why? What did I do?

Zhou-wei:　Not kill you, kill you for an ice cream.

Kate:　　　What are you talking about?

Zhou-wei:　I mean I want an ice cream — you know, kill someone for an ice cream.

Kate:　　　You could kill for an ice cream. Wow, you need to be careful about what you say.

Zhou-wei:　Sorry.

凱特：今天的天氣還真熱啊！
周偉：我能體會，為了一盒冰淇淋要我殺了你都行。
凱特：殺我？為什麼？我做了什麼？
周偉：不是真的殺你，是為了能得到冰淇淋要我做什麼都可以，甚至

是殺了你。

凱特：你到底在說些什麼？

周偉：我的意思是我想要一盒冰淇淋，你知道的，為了冰淇淋「不顧一切」。

凱特：你可以為了一盒冰淇淋而「不顧一切」去做任何事。喔，你得要小心你說的話。

周偉：抱歉。

在上述的例子中，我們學到的是不要害怕使用片語，但你要確認你記得的片語是正確的，以避免造成困惑。

☑ 完全了解片語的意思再使用

第二個須要注意的地方是片語的意思。也就是說，你在使用片語之前要確定你完全了解它的意思。片語可以增加你的文采，所以我會建議你使用，但記得先搞懂意思之後再使用。

這使我想起以前學中文時，老師說過的一則故事。有一個外國學生正在學「愈……，愈……」這個句型，他迫切地想要練習這個句型。於是他到了一家川菜餐廳點菜時，他告訴服務生：愈辣愈好。服務生笑了笑並端上他點的菜色，但那道菜實在太辣了，他根本無法下嚥。服務生無奈地說：因為你說愈辣愈好呀！

接下來看一個片語誤用的例子：

• 片語誤用的例子

Qiu-bai:　I can't eat any more. I'm fed up!

Martin:　　Oh, sorry. This is one of my favorite restaurants. I thought you'd like it.

Qiu-bai: It't fine, but I'm really fed up!

Martin: With what?

Qiu-bai: The food. I can't eat any more.

Martin: Then what are you fed up with?

Qiu-bai: The food.

Martin: Oh, never mind.

邱白：我吃不下了。我已經「受夠了」！
馬丁：喔！對不起。這是我最喜愛的餐廳之一。我以為你會喜歡。
邱白：它很好啊！只是我真的「受夠了」！
馬丁：受夠什麼了？
邱白：這些菜啊。我吃不下了。
馬丁：那你到底受夠什麼了？
邱白：這些菜啊。
馬丁：喔，算了。

　　在上述情況中，邱白以為 fed up 的意思是 being full「吃得很撐」。馬丁以為邱白正為了某事而不開心，因為 be fed up 的意思是「受夠了」。他邀請邱白到餐廳吃飯，卻對他朋友的言行感到困惑。其實邱白並沒有不禮貌的意思，他只是不懂這片語的意思罷了。

☑ 如何越來越熟練的使用片語

　　下列幾點可以幫助你避免這樣的情況。首先，仔細研讀本書，特別注意片語的使用情境。接著，寫下一些你喜歡並會嘗試在日常生活中使用的片語。最後，聽聽你的同事、朋友或者電視節目中用

了哪些片語，你所接觸到的情境愈多愈好，如此一來你會更有信心來使用這些片語。

　　如果你聽到你喜歡的片語被使用了好幾次，太棒了，使用這些片語應該不會出錯。如果你沒聽到這些片語，那也沒關係。你仍然可以試著用它們。然而，要按部就班，一次一個片語。使用一個片語並看對方反應如何。如果對方懂得你的意思，你就可以有信心地重複使用這個片語。如果對方不能理解或是臉上有奇怪的表情，你可以詢問對方你的用法是否正確。他們會給你及時的回饋，幫助你更正你所犯的錯誤。

　　切記：適可而止地問問題，千萬不要每隔五分鐘就問。英文為母語的人士可以幫助你改善英文能力，但每次都問問題則會中斷了對話的進行。

　　你應該了解：英文母語人士和你交談時，他們通常不知道你要加強英文時所面臨的挑戰是什麼。雖然許多英文母語人士也學第二外語，但通常都是拉丁語系，諸如西班牙語、法語或是義大利語等。這些語言不論在語言學上或文化上都和英文有著許多相似處。只有少數的人學習亞洲的語言，諸如韓文、中文或日文。沒有面臨過相同的學習挑戰，他們也就不能體會亞洲人在學習英文上的難處。而且，英文母語人士通常也不甚了解現代的亞洲文化，所以他們也沒有太多的相關知識來促進彼此的溝通。

　　這裡有一個方法可以鑑定你在語言上的技巧。測試的方法很簡單，因為你可以用母語來進行。接下來幾天內，觀察周遭的人在什麼場合對你說了哪些事，注意他們說話的正式程度、禮貌程度、以及使用了多少成語。看看在不同的場合中（像是工作場合、商店、餐廳或家中）說話方式有什麼不同。如果你對這樣的「語言偵查工

作」非常有興趣，就把觀察結果寫在圖表上吧。

　　這種練習的好處是可讓你變成一個主動的溝通者。通常，我們把在日常生活中要使用各種不同的片語視為理所當然。但要把英文說得更好，你必須更主動、積極地去留意母語人士的說話態度、語調、語氣以及他們使用的口語英文。這樣的習慣能協助你了解其他國家的文化、並和各式各樣的母語人士交流，進而成為一位成功的溝通者。

Chapter 4
Challenges 挑戰

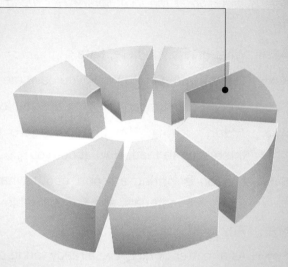

英語學習專欄 ④ 從上下文情境中學習片語

Andrew's 精選對話

🔊 MP3 27

Kate is browsing at the local library. Her friend Sarah approaches her.

Sarah: What brings you here, Kate?

Kate: Oh! It's you, Sarah. Wow, you gave me a fright.

Sarah: Sorry. I didn't mean to. What are you looking for?

Kate: I don't know. I'm just trying to find something interesting to read. How about you?

Sarah: My son is writing a report about whales. He needs to find some materials, and I'm giving him a hand.

Kate: Any luck?

Sarah: As a matter of fact, I've already found several books.

Kate: Great! I hope I can find something. I have to leave soon.

Sarah: Well, I'll leave you to it. Good luck.

翻譯

凱特在當地的圖書館內瀏覽，她的朋友莎拉靠近她。

莎拉：凱特，**妳怎麼會來這裡**？

凱特：喔！是妳呀，莎拉。哇，**妳嚇了我一跳**。

莎拉：對不起，我不是故意的，妳在找什麼書？

凱特：我不知道，我只是想找本有趣的書來讀，妳呢？

莎拉：我兒子正要寫個關於鯨魚的報告，他需要找些資料，而我正在**幫他**找。

凱特：運氣好嗎？

莎拉：**事實上**，我已經找到幾本書了。

凱特：太好了！我希望我可以找到，我得馬上離開了。

莎拉：那麼，**我就讓妳繼續進行吧**，祝妳好運。

進階解析

• I didn't mean to.

「我不是故意的」之意，用來表示之前所做的事是無心的，如：I didn't mean to embarrass you.「我不是故意要讓你難堪的。」

• Any luck?

即為 Have you had any luck?「運氣好嗎？」之意，在文中是詢問對方是不是有那個運氣找到任何她想找的書。這個問句可以在任何時候用來詢問對方做某事是否順利。

① **What brings you here?**

你怎麼會來這裡；什麼風把你吹來了？

例 Welcome, Ms. Reynolds. What brings you here?

歡迎妳，雷諾女士，什麼風把妳吹來了？

---

② **give someone a fright**

嚇了某人一跳

例 You gave me a fright when you slammed the door.

你摔上門的時候嚇了我一跳。

---

③ **give someone a hand**

幫某人的忙

例 Can you give me a hand moving this shelf?

你能幫我搬動這個架子嗎？

---

④ **as a matter of fact**
事實上

例 As a matter of fact, I know exactly what you mean.
事實上，我確實知道你的意思。

⑤ **I'll leave you to it.**
我讓你繼續進行你要做的事。

例 I can see you're busy with work. I'll leave you to it.
我可以看得出來你工作很忙，我會讓你繼續你的工作。

> **Q 進階查詢**
>
> 字面上的字義是「我會把你留給它。」，它指的是對方正在做的事。Leave 本身即有離開的意思，所以整個句意便是「我會離開，讓你去做你正在進行的事情。」

綠字部分為替換語詞，你也可以試著加上更多適當的替換字詞。

①

Sorry. I	didn't mean wasn't trying hadn't planned	to.

對不起，我不是故意的。／不是有意的。／不是有意的。

②

How about What about And	you?

你／你／那你呢？

③

I	have to need to had better	leave soon.

我馬上得／要／要離開了。

✏ Exercises 動手做

A 請由本單元的片語中挑選出適當者，填入下列空格。

1. Listen, I know you've got a lot to do, so I'll _____ it.

2. A: Charles Fields! What _____?
   B: I heard you guys needed some help. I'm here to _____.

3. A: That fall down the stairs gave me _____.
   B: As _____, you're perfectly healthy.

4. Please don't scare me like that. You really gave me a _____.

5. A: Do you have Denise's phone number?
   B: As a _____ of fact, I do.

6. I can see I'm keeping you from work, so I'll _____ you to it.

7. What _____ you here on a Sunday?

8. I want to go, but I have to give my brother a _____ with something.

解答、中譯請見第 231 頁

The Leak

漏水

Andrew's 精選對話

MP3 29

Water is leaking through the ceiling of the Hampsteads' home.

Colleen: Allen, the ceiling's leaking again.

Allen: Again? I just patched it up last week! That stupid ceiling. I can't take it anymore!

Colleen: Get a grip. Hurry up and do something, or the carpet will be ruined!

Allen: Don't have a fit. The carpet will be all right.

Colleen: Not if it keeps getting soaked.

Allen: Find a bucket to catch the water. I'm going to fix that lousy ceiling once and for all.

Colleen: You'd better wait until it stops raining.

Allen: I need at least to cover the area with plastic, to stop the rain from getting in.

Colleen: Give it your best shot, but be careful.

翻譯

罕普司得家的天花板正在漏水。

可琳：阿倫，天花板又在漏水了。

阿倫：又來了？我上個禮拜才把它補好！真是爛天花板，**我再也忍受不了了**！

可琳：**冷靜下來**，快點想個辦法，要不然地毯就要毀了！

阿倫：別**發脾氣**，地毯不會有事的。

可琳：如果它一直泡水就不會沒事。

阿倫：找個水桶來接水吧，我要去修理那個爛天花板了，**一勞永逸**地解決它。

可琳：你還是等到雨停再弄吧。

阿倫：我至少得用塑膠把這個區域遮起來，防止雨水進來。

可琳：**盡力而為**吧，不過要小心。

進階解析

• patch it up

「把某個東西修補好」之意，另外也可以用「patch up+ 情況／關係」來表示「重修舊好某個狀況或某段關係」。

• That stupid ceiling.

Stupid 是用來形容某人事物很差，通常形容的是沒有智慧、無法思考的人事物，如：that stupid car「笨車」、that stupid dog「笨狗」等。

• Not if + S + V

意思為「如果 S 做了 V 就不會……」，這裡的「……」通常是指上個句子裡對方所說的事情。

◉ 核心片語

🎧 MP3 30

① **I can't take it anymore.**

我再也忍受不了了。

例 That noise is making me crazy. I can't take it anymore!

那個噪音快要把我逼瘋了，我再也受不了了！

② **get a grip**

冷靜下來；控制一下你的情緒

例 Get a grip. We need you to stay calm.

冷靜下來，我們需要你保持冷靜。

> ### 🔍 進階查詢
>
> 這個動作是發生在某人因緊張而雙手顫抖時，必須藉著抓住（grip）某樣東西，來穩定自己，因此這個動作所代表的意義就是「冷靜下來」。

③ have a fit
發脾氣；生氣

例 Tory had a fit when Patrick said he didn't like her dress.
當派崔克說他不喜歡托莉的洋裝時，她生氣了。

④ once and for all
一勞永逸；一次就解決它

例 Let's arm wrestle. Once and for all, we'll settle who's stronger.
我們比臂力吧，一次就解決，看誰比較強。

⑤ Give it your best shot.
盡力而為。

例 A: I know I can pass the test.
B: I'm sure you can. Give it your best shot.
A：我知道我能通過測驗的。
B：你當然可以，盡力去做吧。

☑ 精挑句型

綠字部分為替換語詞，你也可以試著加上更多適當的替換字詞。

①

I just	patched it up repaired it had it fixed	last week!

我上個禮拜才把它補好！／修好它！／把它修好！

②

The carpet Everything I'm sure it	will be all right.

地毯／每件事／我確定它都會好好的。

③

You'd better wait until	it stops raining. the rain lets up. the storm breaks.

你還是等到雨停吧。／雨停吧。／暴風雨停了。

✏ Exercises 動手做

A 請由本單元的片語中挑選出適當者，填入下列空格。

1. A: Now we'll finally fix this road once _____.
   B: The noise is making me crazy! I can't take _____.
2. Get _____. Things aren't as bad as they seem.
3. My boyfriend had _____ when I crashed his car.
4. A: Give it _____. We know you can win.
   B: Thank you.

B 選擇正確的字。

1. A: You're driving too fast!
   B: Have/Get a grip. I'm driving under the speed limit.
2. There's no reason to have/start a fit over such a small problem.
3. These weeds keep ruining my garden. I'm going to do something about them once and for finally/all.
4. A: Where are you going? Why are you getting out of the car?
   B: We've been stuck in traffic for two hours. I can't want/take it anymore. I'm walking!
5. A: I'm going to beat you at basketball this time.
   B: Give/Take it your best shot.

解答、中譯請見第 232 頁

A Negative Campaign

負面的競選宣傳

Andrew's 精選對話

🔊 MP3 31

Two friends are watching a commercial from a political campaign.

Paul: Can you believe what he's saying? I don't buy it.

Richard: Neither do I. Three months ago he said he wouldn't run for re-election.

Paul: And now he's giving us a line about how we need him. Give me a break.

Richard: Watch how quickly he breaks all those promises if he's elected.

Paul: Here, here. It's going to be a nasty campaign. They've been going after each other, no holds barred.

Richard: I know. I'm getting tired of politics.

Paul: Me, too. What a world, what a world. Let's watch something else.

Richard: Sure. I'll change the channel.

翻譯

兩個朋友正在看一則政治活動的廣告。

保羅：你相信他說的話嗎？**我可不相信。**

理查：我也不相信，他三個月前才說他不會再出來競選。

保羅：而現在他**騙人**，說我們有多需要他，**別開玩笑了。**

理查：如果他當選了，你看他一定很快就打破他的承諾。

保羅：**我同意**，真是個令人作噁的競選活動，他們一直在**不擇手段**地攻擊別人。

理查：我知道，我對這些政治的東西感到很厭煩了。

保羅：我也是，社會黑暗啊。我們看些別的節目吧。

理查：好啊，我來換台。

進階解析

• run for re-election

字面意思是：為了再次競選而奔走，即「再出來競選」之意。

• go after

「競逐」之意，所以 go after a job「競逐一個工作」、go after a prize「競逐一個獎項」，文中 go after each other 即「互相競逐」。

• tired of + N

「厭倦；厭惡；厭煩某事」之意。

• what a world

有「世風日下、社會黑暗」的涵義在，即「這個世界變差了」，而非「是個好世界」的意思。

① I don't buy it.

我不相信。

例 A: Michael says he wants to be president.

B: I don't buy it. He just wants attention.

A：麥可說他想當總統。

B：我不相信，他只是想引人注意而已吧。

② give someone a line

欺騙某人

例 Can you verify what he said? Are you sure he's not giving you a line?

你能確定他所說的嗎？你確定他沒騙你嗎？

③ Give me a break.

別荒謬了；別開玩笑了；饒了我吧。

例 A: I can do the job by myself.

B: Give me a break. You need all the help you can get.

A：我可以自己做好這個工作。

B：別開玩笑了，你需要所有你可得到的幫助。

④ **Here, here.**

我同意;我有同感。

例 A: It's time we elected a new chairperson.

B: Here, here.

A:該是我們選個新主席的時候了。

B:我有同感。

---

⑤ **no holds barred**

不擇手段

例 During the debate, the opponents challenged each other, no holds barred.

在辯論會中,敵對的雙方不擇手段地挑戰對方。

🔍 **進階查詢**

原本是用在摔角賽中,意思是「怎麼抓都沒有限制」,可以用任何方法使對方輸,所以,引用到生活上,就有「不擇手段」的意思。

☑ 精挑句型

綠字部分為替換語詞，你也可以試著加上更多適當的替換字詞。

①

	what he's saying?
Can you believe	how she spoke to you?
	that outrageous story?

你相信他說的話嗎？／她是怎麼跟你說話的嗎？／那個誇張的故事嗎？

②

	a nasty campaign.
It's going to be	an interesting election.
	a close race.

它將是個令人作噁的競選活動。／有趣的選舉。／勢均力敵的比賽。

③

	tired of	
I'm	getting sick of	**politics.**
	fed up with	

我對這些政治的東西感到很厭煩了。／覺得很厭煩了。／真的受夠了。

✎ **Exercises** 動手做

A 請由本單元的片語中挑選出適當者，填入下列空格。

1. A: This won't hurt at all.
   B: I don't _____. Those drills always hurt.
2. A: With our competitors going after us, no _____, I think you'll all agree these moves are necessary.
   B: Here, _____.
3. A: I'm your daughter's ... um, study partner.
   B: Don't give _____ line. I know you're her new boyfriend.
4. A: I promise I'll get a haircut soon.
   B: _____ break. You've been saying that for weeks.

B 選擇正確的字。

1. The fighters attacked each other, no holds stopped/barred.
2. I don't care what evidence he has. I don't buy/spend it.
3. I'm not lying/giving you a line. I mean what I said.
4. Give/Tell me a break. You know that's not the way the accident happened.
5. A: We need to make going to university more affordable.
   B: Here, yes/here.

解答、中譯請見第 233 頁

從上下文情境中學習片語

☑ 透過上下文學片語，更能掌握如何回應

上下文是了解一個人在說什麼的決定性關鍵。我們所說的每一件事情都有一個特別的背景、或上下文。在真實的世界裡，所有的字與詞都不單獨成為一個片語，在字典裡亦是如此。相反地，它們組合成句子的一部分，也就是二個有某種熟識程度的人之間用來溝通的一部分。

片語就是以這樣的方式被運用在真實世界裡，所以學習片語也應該用同樣的方式，也就是上下文。因為這個理由，本書在一般日常的對話當中運用了許多片語；它們被運用於許許多多不同的情況中。這不但使你知道這些片語在各個特定場合中如何被運用，你也能明白在這些情況下你該如何回應。這是很多片語書沒有做到的。它們也許呈現出片語在一個句子中的用法，但這是不足夠的，你也應該知道要如何回應。

我們來看看下面的例子吧！

Don: **How goes it?**
Hideki: **I'm working.**

唐　　：你近況如何啊！
璽德基：我正在努力工作中。

如果唐問的是 What are you doing?，璽德基的回答才是適當的。但在上面的例子中唐想知道的是璽德基最近過得如何，而不是他現

在正在做什麼。如果璽德基知道片語的意思，也懂得如何回應，就不會犯了上面的錯誤。下面為正確的示範。

Don: **How goes it?**

Hideki: **Same old, same old.**

唐　　：你近況如何啊！

璽德基：一樣，老樣子！

☑ 從不同的情境、不同的例子來學習一個片語

在了解片語如何在對話中自然地被使用後，接著就要了解各個片語的意思，並看看更多的使用範例。這會讓你更了解片語在不同情境下的用法。因此，記住使用的情境是一件重要的事，而且是多多益善。畢竟，不只是片語的學習，學習英文單字也是如此，只讀一個範例是絕對不夠的。因為，多樣的情境範例能作為單字或片語的多種用法的樣本。當學習者對於所學能有更深入的了解，也就能獲得更多的自信了。總而言之，這本書從「精選對話」、「核心片語」到「Exercises 動手做」提供了多種情境作為片語的使用背景，提升讀者對片語使用的熟悉度。

☑ 聽讀同步

研讀本書時，請務必搭配 MP3，這是訓練聽力的絕佳機會。在讀完「精選對話」後，請聽 MP3 練習。第一次聽的時候，請對照著書。第二次時，請把書闔上，專心聽就好，聽聽句子的語調、以及片語與其他字如何銜接。

若是你能按照此方式研讀本書，對於你理解英語人士們所使用的片語是相當有助益的。

☑ 練習

　　學會了片語在口說英語中的使用方式後，就需要透過一些練習來測試你的學習成效。「Exercises 動手做」單元即提供了這樣的練習，這些練習都是一般人在生活中真正會使用的英文。

☑ 複習

　　複習是英文學習中重要的一環，但卻最容易被忽略。無論你學的是購物所需的單字、或者是旅遊時所需的句子、還是在飛機上的措詞表達，經常性地複習你所學過的東西是一件重要的事。

　　通常，語言學習者都會急著在短時間內盡可能地多學一些單字與句型。這當然是值得讚許的目標，不過，沒那麼幸運的是，學習語言不像是搭乘新幹線一樣可以直線行駛，而是你必須進入一種固定的學習模式中，不管是單字或是片語，都要培養出自己的學習方法，然後不斷地回頭檢視，才能再吸收下個單字或片語。

　　我建議大家在研讀本書中的四或五個單元後，重新再讀一次「精選對話」，看看你對所學過片語的涵義記得多少。如果需要，可以將你學到的片語列出來，每天看一次。在開始讀新單元之前，也可以回頭看看曾經學過的所有片語。當你對某個片語非常熟悉時，可以把它從你的列表中刪除，針對你比較無法掌握的片語多下些功夫。

Chapter 5
Daily Life 日常生活

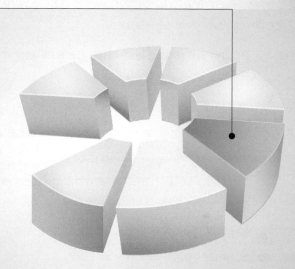

英語學習專欄 ⑤ 學習片語的要領

Andrew's 精選對話

(◎) MP3 33

It's 6:45, past the end of the work day. Everyone has left the office, except for two colleagues.

Jeff: I think we're the last ones here. Want to call it quits?

Shirley: For sure. I'm exhausted.

Jeff: At least we got most everything done.

Shirley: True, but I'd like to go over the case again. We don't want to make any mistakes.

Jeff: I'm with you there. If anything goes wrong, our necks are on the line.

Shirley: Exactly. So I'll see you early tomorrow morning.

Jeff: Sounds good. Catch you later.

Shirley: Bye.

翻譯

六點四十五分，已經過了下班時間，除了兩位同事外，其他人都離開辦公室了。

傑夫：我想我們是最後走的人，我們就**歇手吧**。

雪莉：**當然囉**，我已經累壞了。

傑夫：至少我們完成了大部分的事。

雪莉：對啊，不過我還是想再把這個案子看一遍，我們可不想有任何的疏失。

傑夫：**我同意**，如果有任何事出錯，**我們得負責的**。

雪莉：完全正確，那麼，明天一早再見。

傑夫：好，**再見**。

雪莉：拜拜。

進階解析

● at least

「至少；最少」之意，如：At least you fed the fish, or Mom would be real angry.「最起碼你有餵魚，不然媽真的會很生氣。」

● go over

「看過；做過；經過」某事物的動作，如：If you don't mind, I would like to go over the report again.「如果你不介意的話，我想再看一次這個報告。」

● Sounds good.

即 That sounds good.，只是將 That 省略，英文中有很多類似的說法。

● Catch you later.

即 See you later.，Catch 有「接收到；看到」的意思，Catch you later. 是「回頭見；再見」的意思。

① **call it quits**

歇手；罷手；停止做某事

例 Does anybody else want to call it quits now?

還有誰想要現在停工的嗎？

② **For sure.**

絕對；當然；一定

例 A: That movie was the best!

B: For sure.

A：那部電影是最棒的！

B：那當然。

③ **I'm with you there.**

我同意。

例 A: Prices are just too high at this store.

B: I'm with you there.

A：這家店的物價太高了。

B：我同意。

④ **someone's neck is on the line**

某人對某事有責任

例 Remember, my neck is on the line, so be careful.

記得，我得為這事情負責，所以小心一點。

> **Q 進階查詢**
>
> line 是指斷頭台上鍘刀所切過的那條線，意思就是「某人的脖子正在斷頭台上待鍘」，用來引引申為「準備受過；得為某事負責」的意思。

⑤ **Catch you later.**

再見。

例 I've got to go. I'll catch you later.

我得走了，再見。

綠字部分為替換語詞，你也可以試著加上更多適當的替換字詞。

①

At least we	got most everything done. finished almost everything. took care of most of our work.

至少我們做完了大部分的事。／幾乎完成了每件事。／處理完我們大部分的工作。

②

True, but I'd like to	go over the case review it look at it	again.

對啊，不過我還是想再把這個案子看一遍。／重看一遍。／看一遍。

③

So I'll see you	early tomorrow morning. later this evening. some time this weekend.

那麼，明天一早／傍晚晚一點／這個週末找個時候我們再見。

✏ Exercises 動手做

A 請由本單元的片語中挑選出適當者，填入下列空格。

1. Johnson, I hope you know that if you mess up, your neck
   _____.

2. A: I don't think we should call _____ until we're finished.

   B: I'm with _____. We have to finish today.

3. A: This cake is going to be great!

   B: For _____! Your cooking is always good.

4. A: I'm going home. Catch _____.

   B: Bye!

5. A: Good bye, Peter.

   B: _____, Timothy.

6. Please be careful, since this is my friend's house. If you break anything, my _____.

7. A: Isn't this CD great?

   B: _____. It's their best CD to date.

8. You've already lost a lot of money. You should _____.

9. A: I think we should go to another club.

   B: I'm _____. This one's full of smoke.

解答、中譯請見第 233 頁

Let's Go Out for Dinner.

我們出去吃晚餐。

Andrew's 精選對話

MP3 35

Chris calls his girlfriend on the phone. He has some good news.

Lisa: Hello?

Chris: Hey, you. What's happening?

Lisa: Nothing, as usual. I was just taking it easy.

Chris: Listen to this. I just won fifty bucks in the lottery.

Lisa: Get out of here! Are you jerking my string?

Chris: No, I'm serious.

Lisa: That's great. You are so lucky.

Chris: Let's go out to dinner tonight. My treat.

Lisa: How sweet. Pick me up at 7:00.

翻譯

克里斯打電話給他的女朋友，有好消息告訴她。

莉莎　　：喂？

克里斯：嗨，**妳在做什麼**？

莉莎　　：沒什麼，跟往常一樣，我剛剛在**放鬆休息一下**。

克里斯：妳聽我說，我剛剛贏了五十塊錢的樂透獎金。

莉莎　　：**我不相信**！你在**開我玩笑**嗎？

克里斯：沒有，我說真的。

莉莎　　：那太棒了，你好幸運。

克里斯：我們今天出去吃晚餐吧，**我請客**。

莉莎　　：你真好，七點來接我吧。

進階解析

• Hey, you.

這個招呼語是非正式的，只用在非常要好的朋友之間，跟普通朋友不會使用這樣的用語，因為會被視為無禮或缺乏尊重。

• I was just + V-ing

用來表示「我只是在做……而已，沒做別的。」例如：I was just listening to music when you came home.「你回來時，我只是在聽聽音樂，沒做別的事。」

• How sweet.

How + adj. 用來表示對方「真的很……」，例：How beautiful.「真美」、How wonderful.「真是太好了」、How stupid.「真笨」。

① **What's happening?**

你在做些什麼？

例 What's happening, guys?

夥伴們，你們在幹嘛？

② **take it easy**

放輕鬆

例 Take it easy while I find out what's going on.

在我弄清楚發生了什麼事的時候，你可以輕鬆一下。

③ **Get out of here.**

少來了，我不信；不可能。

例 A: I'm going on a cruise around the world.

B: Get out of here!

A：我就要搭著郵輪環遊世界了。

B：你別騙人了，我不相信。

Q　　進階查詢

並不是真的叫人滾開，而是當對方有令人難以相信的事情發生時，我們會覺得那是不可能的，並笑鬧地叫對方馬上從我們面前消失，藉以表達我們覺得「不可能」的感覺。

④ **jerk someone's string**

誤導某人；愚弄某人

例 This is serious, so you'd better not be jerking my string.

事態很嚴重，所以你最好別開我玩笑。

⑤ **my treat**

我付錢；我請客

例 You paid last time. This time, it's my treat.

你上次付過了，這次，該我請客。

☑ 精挑句型

綠字部分為替換語詞，你也可以試著加上更多適當的替換字詞。

①

I was	taking it easy. just relaxing. watching TV.

我剛剛在輕鬆一下。／放鬆一下。／看電視。

②

I just won fifty bucks	in the lottery. playing poker. in Las Vegas.

我剛剛玩樂透／玩撲克牌／在拉斯維加斯贏了五十塊錢。

③

Let's Why don't we We should	go out to dinner tonight.

今天晚上我們／我們何不／我們應該出去吃飯。

✏ Exercises 動手做

A 請由本單元的片語中挑選出適當者，填入下列空格。

1. A: This dress is $300.
   B: _____ of here. I thought it was on sale.

2. A: Are you jerking _____? You're really quitting your job?
   B: Take _____. I haven't decided for sure yet.

3. A: Hi, Fred. What's _____?
   B: Good morning, Jed. I was thinking of taking our families out to dinner. My _____.

4. Take it _____. I was only joking around.

5. After dinner, I'm taking you all out for ice cream. My _____.

6. I knew you were _____ my string.

7. What's _____, everybody?

8. You just got promoted to manager? Get _____ of here!

解答、中譯請見第 234 頁

Now, What?

那現在要怎麼樣？

Andrew's 精選對話　　　　　🄫 MP3 37

Seth and Thomas graduated from university a week ago. They're talking at a coffee shop.

Seth: Can you believe we finally graduated? It's pretty weird.

Thomas: I know where you're coming from. I'm still not used to it.

Seth: No tests, no essays, no reports. Man, now what am I going to do?

Thomas: Beats me. I want to do something important, you know?

Seth: Yeah, but what?

Thomas: I'm not sure yet. See, I want a job I can enjoy and make money from.

Seth: Easier said than done. I was thinking of joining the Peace Corps.

Thomas: No way! Are you serious?

Seth: It's one possibility.

Thomas: Man, that's a trip. But it would be a pretty cool job.

翻譯

席斯和湯瑪士一週前從大學畢業了，他們在一家咖啡店裡聊天。

席斯 ：你能相信我們終於畢業了嗎？感覺好奇怪。

湯瑪士：**我知道你的意思**，我還沒辦法習慣。

席斯 ：沒有考試、沒有論文、沒有報告。天啊，接下來的日子我要做些什麼啊？

湯瑪士：**我不知道。**我想做些有重大意義的事，你了解嗎？

席斯 ：我了解，不過你要做什麼呢？

湯瑪士：我還不確定。你看，我想找一個做得很愉快又可以賺錢的工作。

席斯 ：**說的比做的容易。**我才在想說要加入和平組織。

湯瑪士：**不可能吧！**你是認真的嗎？

席斯 ：那是一種可能。

湯瑪士：老兄，**那真令人驚訝**，不過那會是個很酷的工作。

進階解析

• See, I want a job I can enjoy.

See 即 You see，並不是真的要對方看什麼，而是請對方聽接下來要說或解釋的狀況。

• Peace Corps

美國幫助貧苦國家為目的的和平組織，和台灣的世界展望會類似，加入 Peace Corps 的人會到各個貧窮國家去從事兩三年與教育、農業、建設等有關的工作，雖然是義工性質，Peace Corps 還是會在你離開後給你薪水。

① **I know where you're coming from.**

我知道你的意思。

例 A: Sometimes it's hard to make decisions like this.

B: I know where you're coming from.

A：有時候很難做出像這樣的決定。

B：我知道你的意思。

> **Q** 進階查詢
>
> 字面意思為「我知道你從哪裡來」，表示我知道你的根源，既然知道對方的底細，就能了解對方在說些什麼了，所以引申為「我了解你的意思」之意。

② **Beats me.**

我不知道；問倒我了。

例 A: Who's going to be our new manager?

B: Beats me.

A：誰會是我們的新經理？

B：問倒我了。

③ **Easier said than done.**

說的比做的容易。

例 I know you want to be a great chef, but that's easier said than done.

我知道你想成為一個很棒的廚師，不過說的比做的簡單。

④ **No way!**

不可能；少來；你沒開玩笑吧！

例 A: I talked with the president on the phone.

B: No way!

A：我跟總統講電話。

B：少來了！

⑤ **That's a trip.**

那真令人驚訝。

例 You wife's going to have twins? Wow, that's a trip.

你的老婆懷了雙胞胎嗎？哇，那真令人驚訝。

☑ 精挑句型

綠字部分為替換語詞，你也可以試著加上更多適當的替換字詞。

①

	we finally graduated?
Can you believe	we have to find a job?
	four years went by so fast?

你能相信我們終於畢業了嗎？／我們得去找工作嗎？／四年這麼快就過去了嗎？

②

	weird.
It's pretty	strange.
	amazing.

那真奇怪。／奇怪。／令人驚訝。

③

	joining the Peace Corps.
I was thinking of	traveling around the world.
	doing volunteer work.

我在考慮加入和平組織。／環遊世界。／去當義工。

✎ **Exercises** 動手做

A 請由本單元的片語中挑選出適當者，填入下列空格。

1. A: Prices keep going up on this stuff.
   B: I know _____ from.

2. A: You should quit drinking coffee.
   B: Hah! That's easier _____.

3. A: See here. I used to be popular with the ladies.
   B: _____ way! Is that you?
   C: Wow, that's _____. You've changed a lot.

4. A: What do you think these dreams mean?
   B: _____ me.

5. A: I inherited $50,000.
   B: No _____!

6. A: When is their new CD coming out?
   B: _____ me.

7. A: Can you believe what happened?
   B: Yeah, that's a _____.

8. Getting all this done today is _____ said than done.

9. A: But, I don't want to move.
   B: I know where you're _____ from.

解答、中譯請見第 235 頁

Andrew's 精選對話

MP3 39

Brad and Janie are at a restaurant. After they have waited for forty-five minutes, their food finally arrives.

Brad: This soup is cold! Now I'm really ticked off!

Janie: Relax, Brad. There's no reason to lose your temper.

Brad: No reason to ... we've been sitting here close to an hour, and they expect us to eat cold food?

Janie: Will you please drop it? You're making a scene.

Brad: Good. This place needs to learn they can't treat their guests like garbage.

Janie: Maybe we should just leave.

Brad: That's not good enough. I want to talk to the manager. I'll give him a piece of my mind.

翻譯

布萊德和潔妮在一家餐廳裡。等了四十五分鐘後，他們點的食物終於來了。

布萊德：這個湯是冷的！現在，我真的**火大了**！

潔妮　：輕鬆點，布萊德。沒有理由**發脾氣**的。

布萊德：沒有理由……我們已經坐在這兒等了將近一個小時，他們還期望我們會吃冷掉的食物嗎？

潔妮　：可不可以請你**別說了**？你**把場面搞得很尷尬**。

布萊德：好，這個地方得學學，他們不能把客人當垃圾看待。

潔妮　：也許我們應該就走了算了。

布萊德：那還不夠，我要跟他們的經理談談，我要**讓他知道我真正的想法**。

🔖 進階解析

• no reason to + V

「沒有理由……」，例：Brad Pitt is just another human being. There's no reason to lose your mind when you see him on TV.「布萊德‧彼特不過是另一個人類而已，你在電視上看到他時，沒有理由失去理智吧。」

• treat + someone + like garbage

「把某人當垃圾一樣對待」，例：The clerks at that clothes store treat people without gorgeous outfits like garbage.「那家服飾店的店員把衣著不光鮮的客人當垃圾一樣對待。」

① **ticked off**

生氣；火大

例 Tom got ticked off when a guy at work spilled coffee on his desk.

上班時有個人把咖啡灑在湯姆的桌上惹得他很火大。

② **lose one's temper**

生氣；發脾氣

例 This traffic had better clear up soon. I'm about to lose my temper.

交通最好趕快順暢起來，我快要發脾氣了。

③ **drop it**

別說了；別再說了

例 A: You shouldn't have sold your car.

B: I said drop it. I don't want to talk about it any more.

A：你不該把你的車賣掉。

B：我說你別再說了，我不想再談這件事了。

④ **make a scene**

把場面搞得尷尬

例 Lower your voice. You're making a scene.

小聲一點，你正把場面弄得很尷尬。

⑤ **give someone a piece of one's mind**

告訴他人某人心裡的真正想法

例 That new guy is too arrogant. I'm going to give him a piece of my mind.

那個新來的太傲慢了，我要讓他知道我心裡真正的想法。

> 🔍 **進階查詢**
>
> 意謂著把某人心思的一部分拿出來給另一個人，以便讓那個人知道某人心裡在想些什麼。

綠字部分為替換語詞，你也可以試著加上更多適當的替換字詞。

①

This	soup food beef	is cold.

這個湯／食物／牛肉是冷的。

②

We've been sitting here	close to an hour. for a long time. since 12:45.

我們已經坐在這兒將近一個小時。／好久了。／從十二點四十五分開始。

③

Maybe we should I think we should We ought to	just leave.

也許我們應該／我想我們應該／我們應該就走了算了。

✏️ Exercises 動手做

A 請由本單元的片語中挑選出適當者，填入下列空格。

1. A: I think you should ＿＿＿＿＿＿ it, or you may get into trouble at work.

   B: I don't care. I'm going to give my boss ＿＿＿＿＿＿.

2. A: People say you lose ＿＿＿＿＿＿ over small things. Is that true?

   B: I guess so. I get angry easily.

3. A: Now I'm ＿＿＿＿＿＿ off. You need to learn a lesson.

   B: If you want to make ＿＿＿＿＿＿, that's fine. I'm not running away from you.

4. A: Let's talk about it some more.

   B: No. And I'd appreciate it if you'd just ＿＿＿＿＿＿.

5. When I saw Steve's angry expression, I knew he was ＿＿＿＿＿＿.

6. Tyler lost ＿＿＿＿＿＿ when I told him what Joe said.

7. Everyone's looking at us. Why did you have to ＿＿＿＿＿＿?

8. A: You shouldn't let Kramer talk to you that way.

   B: You're right. The next time I see him, I'm going to give ＿＿＿＿＿＿.

解答、中譯請見第 236 頁

Andrew's 精選對話

MP3 41

For years, Cecilia has been unhappy with her nose. Now, she's doing something about it.

Kelly: Did you say you're getting a nose job?

Cecilia: Quiet! I don't want to advertise it to the world.

Kelly: But your nose looks fine.

Cecilia: It does not. It's huge, like a pear.

Kelly: OK, so you don't like your nose. But getting an operation is a bit over the top, don't you think?

Cecilia: I thought you'd back me up. You're supposed to be my friend.

Kelly: I am. I wish I could talk some sense into you.

Cecilia: My decision's final. Now, can you help me choose a nose from this catalog?

Kelly: If you insist.

翻譯

瑟西莉亞不滿意她自己的鼻子好多年了，如今，她終於要有所行動。

凱莉 　　：妳說妳要動鼻子整型手術？

瑟西莉亞：小聲一點，我可不想**大肆宣揚**。

凱莉 　　：不過，妳的鼻子看起來挺好的啊。

瑟西莉亞：才不呢，我的鼻子很大，像個梨子似的。

凱莉 　　：好吧，看來妳是不喜歡妳的鼻子，不過，動手術未免有點**太過火了**，妳不覺得嗎？

瑟西莉亞：我還以為妳會**支持我**，妳應該是我的朋友吧。

凱莉 　　：我是啊，我只希望我能夠**讓妳清醒點**。

瑟西莉亞：我心意已決。現在，妳能幫我從這個目錄中挑選一個鼻型嗎？

凱莉 　　：**如果妳堅持的話**。

🔖 進階解析

● a nose job

對鼻子做些事，就是「幫鼻子做些改變」。除了鼻子外，在整容方面也有 a chin job「下巴的整容」或 face lift「拉皮」等。

● getting an operation is a bit …

「Ving + N + is + adj.」意思為「做……是……的」，如：Playing video games is always fun.「玩電視遊樂器一直都是很好玩的。」

● My decision's final.

「N + is final.」意思為「某件事已成定局，無法改變了。」

⊚ 核心片語

① **advertise something to the world**
讓很多人知道

例 A: You're getting divorced?
B: Keep your voice down. I don't want to advertise it to the world.
A：你要離婚啦？
B：小聲點，我可不想大肆張揚。

② **over the top**
過分；太誇張

例 Many people felt the politician's statements were over the top.
很多人都覺得政客的說辭太誇張了。

③ **back someone up**
支持某人

例 Can you please back me up on this?
在這件事情上你能支持我嗎？

④ **talk sense into someone**

讓某人認清事實

例 I've tried, but I've been unable to talk any sense into him.

我試過了，不過我就是沒辦法讓他聽進去。

> **Q 進階查詢**
>
> 將某些道理灌輸給某人，試著讓某人接受別人說的話，所以就有「跟某人講道理」的意思。

⑤ **If you insist.**

如果你堅持的話；好吧。

例 A: But I really want you to go with me.

B: If you insist.

A：但我真的想要你跟我一起去嘛。

B：好啦，好啦。

> **Q 進階查詢**
>
> 這個片語可指某人同意做某事，或同意某事實或說辭；有時也用來結束一段不甚愉快的談話，來讓對方住口。

☑ 精挑句型

綠字部分為替換語詞，你也可以試著加上更多適當的替換字詞。

①

Did you say	you're getting a nose job? you want to have plastic surgery? it's going to cost $5,000?

你說你要給你的鼻子整容嗎？／你想要動整型手術嗎？／那要花五千塊錢嗎？

②

You're supposed to	be my friend. support me. agree with me.

你應該是我的朋友吧。／要支持我吧。／要同意我吧。

③

My decision's	final. made. set.

我心意已決。／已決。／已決。

✎ Exercises 動手做

A 請由本單元的片語中挑選出適當者，填入下列空格。

1. What do you mean, I'll being over _____? I'm going to talk _____ if it's the last thing I do.

2. A: Hey, your new hair piece looks great!
   B: I wish you wouldn't _____ the world.

3. A: Now, when we talk to Johnson, don't forget to _____ up. I need your support.
   B: If _____. I hope you know what you're doing.

B 選擇正確的字。

1. Can you help me talk some sense/right into my daughter?

2. Why is it that nobody will support/back me up?

3. Many critics feel the proposal is past/over the top.

4. Now, don't tell anybody else. I don't want to market/ advertise this to the world.

5. I'll do it, if you insist/demand. But I'm not happy about it.

解答、中譯請見第 236 頁

學習片語的要領

☑ 了解片語的來源，更容易記住

　　了解一個片語的來源可以幫助我們對片語產生興趣，也有助於我們對每個片語的了解。以 life in the fast line「刺激的生活」為例（書中將會介紹），它的字面意思為「快車道上的生活」，那為何會有「刺激的生活」的涵意呢？快車道是專門為開車較快的人所設計的，他們生活步調較快、也較能適應新鮮刺激的事物。所以當人們「生活在快車道上」，指的就是他們能夠去嘗試新的挑戰和接受較新鮮的生活方式。

　　藉著了解一個片語的背景，可以加深你對這個片語的印象，使你更容易記得它。了解一個片語的起源，也能夠讓你進一步去探索這個片語在文化上的精髓和價值。例 Keep your chin up「保持一個正面的態度」。一般人心情不佳或是處於低潮的時候，都會垂頭喪氣，而這樣的情緒也會明顯地表現在臉上。肢體語言可以傳達我們的感受給予他人。當我們建議他人 Keep your chin up，我們給予他的不只是字面上（把下巴抬高）同時也是深層涵義上（保持正面的態度）的建議。

　　本書的「進階查詢」單元即在解釋這些片語的來源。

☑ 透過自己生產的句子，強化對單字、片語的學習效果

　　目前，我已經嘗過學習六種語言的樂趣。是哪幾種語言呢？中文、日文、西班牙文、法文、德文以及英文。有些我可以說得很好，有些則只是在基礎階段。主要的原因還是歸於所花時間的多寡，以

及練習的次數。總之，對所學過的每一種語言，我都養成了一個習慣，就是寫句子。

我會用個本子記下所學到的新字彙。也會依照俚語、成語、或其他的語言型態來分門別類。單字或片語就寫在頁面的左邊，然後接著寫下詞性，再來是解釋。同一行（若沒有空間就寫在下一行）我會寫下我所造的句子，不需要是很複雜的句子，只要能夠證明自己會用這個字，重要的是我不是從書上照抄句子。任何人都會抄，但自己造句能夠增強對單字或片語的認識，並且使我更主動地去學習。（以一個和句子一樣長的片語為例，我會寫上兩行長度的對話：一句包含那個片語；另一句則是我自己所造的句子。）

基本上我每天都會把筆記複習一遍。為了要測驗自己的學習成果，我會把解釋的地方先遮起來，然後看看自己是否理解這些單字和片語。接下來，我會拿出一張空白的紙，利用這些單字、片語造句。如果單字很多，我會挑選幾個來造句子。句子可長可短，可以是嚴肅也可以是有趣的，也可以是關於任何主題的。我每天都會花上至少二十到三十分鐘作練習，因為我認為這是學習語言最重要的部分。如果你沒那麼多時間，就每天花五至十分鐘，在公車、捷運上、或是吃早餐時，寫下一些句子。重要的是養成習慣。慢慢你就會發現自己寫下了生活中各種有趣的事，那些發生在工作上、或是新聞中的事。最令人感到興奮的是，你可是用英文寫的喔！

Chapter 6

Relationships 關係

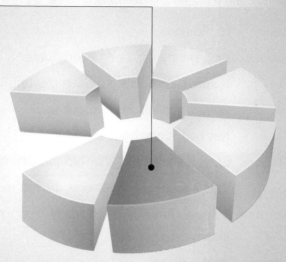

Andrew's 精選對話

MP3 43

Danny and Ramona are old friends. They see each other at a party.

Danny: Hi, Ramona.

Ramona: Hey, Danny. It's been a long time.

Danny: It sure has. How's life been treating you?

Ramona: Can't complain. How about you?

Danny: Not bad, since I got a new job.

Ramona: So you finally quit your old job. It's about time.

Danny: That's a fact. My boss was driving me crazy.

Ramona: I know. Anyway, it is really good to see you again, Danny.

Danny: Yeah, you too.

翻譯

丹尼和雷蒙娜是老朋友，他們在舞會遇到對方。

丹尼　：嗨，雷蒙娜。

雷蒙娜：嗨，丹尼，**好久不見**。

丹尼　：是很久沒見面了，**妳過得怎樣**？

雷蒙娜：**不錯**，你呢？

丹尼　：不錯啊，因為我找到新工作了。

雷蒙娜：所以你終於辭掉了舊工作，**該是時候了**。

丹尼　：那倒也是，我老闆快**把我逼瘋了**。

雷蒙娜：我知道，不管怎樣，我真的很高興見到你，丹尼。

丹尼　：也很高興見到妳。

🖈 進階解析

• It's been a long time.

即 It's been a long time since I've seen you.「自從我上次見到你後已經過了很長一段時間」，意即「好久不見」。

• Can't complain.

即 I can't complain.，將主詞 I 省略了，字面意思為「我無法抱怨」，無可抱怨之處，也就有「還好；不錯」的意思。

• It's about time.

「該是時候了」，指的是對方之前所說的事。文中，雷蒙娜所指的就是丹尼換新工作之事。

① **It's been a long time.**

好久不見。

例 How are you, Jack? It's been a long time.

你好嗎，傑克？好久不見了。

② **How's life been treating you?**

近來如何；你好嗎？

例 A: Hi, Patty. How's life been treating you?

B: So-so.

A：嗨，派蒂，近來如何啊？

B：馬馬虎虎。

> **Q** 進階查詢
>
> 「生活如何對待你，是不是讓你好過」來詢問對方，即是問候對方「最近的生活過得如何，是否被生活所累」。

③ Can't complain.

還好；還不錯。

例 A: How are you?
B: Can't complain.

A：你好嗎？

B：還不錯。

④ It's about time.

終於；該是時候了。

例 You're finally here. It's about time.

你終於到了，也該是時候了。

⑤ driving someone crazy

嚴重干擾某人；把某人逼瘋

例 This music is driving me crazy.

這個音樂快要讓我抓狂了。

☑ 精挑句型

綠字部分為替換語詞，你也可以試著加上更多適當的替換字詞。

①

So you finally	quit left got tired of	your old job.

所以你終於辭掉／離開／厭倦你的舊工作了。

②

That's	a fact. for sure. true.

那是事實。／想當然爾。／真的。

③

My boss was	driving me crazy. making my job unpleasant. treating me unfairly.

我老闆快要把我逼瘋了。／讓我工作得不愉快。／對我不公平。

✏ Exercises 動手做

A 請由本單元的片語中挑選出適當者，填入下列空格。

1. A: Hello, Annie. It's been _____.
   B: Yes, it has. I haven't seen you for four or five years.

2. A: Hi, Phil. How's life _____?
   B: Oh, I can't _____. Everything's going all right.

3. A: Will you please stop making stupid jokes? You're driving _____.
   B: Sorry. I thought you liked my jokes.

4. A: So you finally got promoted.
   B: Right. It's _____. I've been waiting for years.

B 選擇正確的字。

1. You're finally getting married? It's about/around time.

2. I'm so glad to see you. It's been a much/long time.

3. Living in the city drives/rides me crazy sometimes.

4. A: Are you doing all right?
   B: I can't/won't complain.

5. Welcome to the party, Mr. Reed. How's life it's/been treating you?

解答、中譯請見第 237 頁

Andrew's 精選對話

MP3 45

Tory and Dave are going out together, but they just had a fight. Tory's brother, Chad, wants to talk with Dave.

Chad: My sister is at home crying right now. What have you got to say?

Dave: I say mind your own business.

Chad: You want me to mind my own business? Why don't I just mop up the floor with you?

Dave: You and what army?

Chad: I wouldn't need an army to take care of you.

Dave: Aw, you're full of hot air. Relax, Rambo.

Chad: Listen, Dave. I want you to stay away from my sister.

Dave: Let's get something straight. I do what I want, when I want, and with whoever I want.

翻譯

朵麗和戴夫在交往，不過他們剛吵了一架。朵麗的哥哥查德想跟戴夫談一談。

查德：我妹現在正在家裡哭，你有什麼話說？

戴夫：我說**你少管閒事**。

查德：你要我少管閒事？那我**痛扁你一頓**如何？

戴夫：**就憑你嗎**？

查德：我不用別人幫忙就可以收拾你。

戴夫：哦，你是在**虛張聲勢**吧，放輕鬆點，藍波。

查德：你給我聽著，戴夫，我要你離我妹妹遠一點。

戴夫：**讓我們把話挑明了講吧**，我想跟誰在什麼時候做什麼事，誰都管不著。

進階解析

● What have you got to say?

即 What have you got to say for yourself?「你有什麼好說的；你有什麼說辭來為自己辯駁？」，用來要求對方給個合理的解釋。

● take care of you

不是「照顧對方」，而是要「收拾對方」的用語，在閩南語中也有相同的用語「我會好好地給你照顧」，語言雖不同，卻都表達相同的意思。

● Rambo

為美國文化的產物，取自藍波系列電影，因為藍波可以以一己之力打擊諸多對手，所以便被引用來形容「不需要別人幫助就可打倒對方的強人」，此處有戲謔對方的意味。

① **mind one's own business**
管好自己就好；少管閒事

例 Some people have trouble minding their own business.
有些人就是沒有辦法不管閒事。

② **mop up the floor with someone**
海扁某人一頓

例 Shane threatened to mop up the floor with Sal.
尚恩威脅要海扁薩爾一頓。

③ **You and what army?**
就憑你嗎；你跟你的哪些幫手啊？（有示威的語氣）

例 A: You'd better learn some manners, or I'll teach you some!
B: Oh yeah? You and what army?
A：你最好學點規矩，不然我可要教教你了！
B：哦，是嗎？就憑你嗎？

> ◒ — 進階查詢
>
> 用「你跟什麼軍隊」來暗指對方需要一個軍隊的協助才能和自己抗衡，言下之意就是對方實力很弱，需要別人的幫忙。跟中文的「就憑你嗎？」的意思是一樣的。

④ **full of hot air**

打腫臉充胖子；虛張聲勢；外表強硬，內心軟弱

例 Don't worry about Terrance. He's full of hot air.

別擔心達倫斯，他只是虛張聲勢而已。

⑤ **Let's get something straight.**

我們把話說清楚。

例 Let's get something straight. I'm the leader of this expedition.

我們把話說清楚吧，這趟旅行我是老大。

綠字部分為替換語詞，你也可以試著加上更多適當的替換字詞。

①

You want me to	mind my own business? keep out of this? leave you alone?

你要我少管閒事？／別管這件事？／別管你？

②

Listen, Listen to me, I'm warning you,	Dave.

你聽著，／給我聽著，／我警告你，戴夫。

③

I want you to	stay away from keep away from stop calling	my sister.

我要你別再來騷擾／遠離／別再打電話給我妹妹。

✏ Exercises 動手做

A 請由本單元的片語中挑選出適當者，填入下列空格。

1. A: I'm gonna _____ with you.

   B: Ouch! From now on, I'd better mind _____.

2. So he said, "Let's _____. I'm the boss." And I said, "Not anymore. I quit."

3. A: I can beat anyone stupid enough to get me mad.

   B: You and _____?

   C: That guy is _____ air.

4. A: Stop it, or I'll beat you up.

   B: You _____?

5. That guy's huge. He could _____ us.

6. No, I will not _____. I want to know what happened.

7. Let's _____. I'm the boss around here.

8. Allen's _____. He wouldn't hurt a fly.

解答、中譯請見第 238 頁

Andrew's 精選對話

MP3 47

Aaron and Larry are having lunch at their school's cafeteria.

Larry: Look, Aaron, there's Trisha Fry. Go ask her out.

Aaron: No. I don't want to.

Larry: Don't give me that. I know you do. Or are you afraid?

Aaron: Don't make me laugh. I'm just not in the mood to ask her out.

Larry: Mama's boy, mama's boy — afraid to talk to a girl.

Aaron: Cut it out. I'm not a mama's boy.

Larry: Prove it.

Aaron: Fine. I'll go talk to her right now.

翻譯

阿倫和賴瑞在學校的自助餐廳裡吃午餐。

賴瑞：阿倫，你看，范翠莎在那邊，去約她出去。

阿倫：不要，我不想。

賴瑞：**你隨口說說的吧**，我知道你想要的，要不然就是你在害怕囉？

阿倫：**別荒謬了**，我只是沒那個**心情**去約她。

賴瑞：膽小鬼，膽小鬼，害怕跟女生說話。

阿倫：**別鬧了**，我才不是膽小鬼。

賴瑞：證明啊。

阿倫：好，我現在就去跟她說。

進階解析

• **mama's boy**

意即「媽媽的小男孩」，指的就是還黏著媽媽、長不大的小孩，在對話中用來指對方是「膽小懦弱還需要母親保護的人」。

• **afraid to**

在文中並沒有主詞，口語中常有這種沒有主詞的句子，通常是發生動作的主詞已經非常明顯時，就把主詞省略掉。

• **Prove it.**

「證明它」。當我們希望對方證明某件事時，這句話就很好用。

例 Phil:　That's nothing fancy. I can do that magic trick, too.

Jean:　Prove it.

菲爾：那不算什麼，我也會變那種把戲。

琴　：那就證明啊。

① **ask someone out**

約某人出去

例 I asked Amy out to a movie.

我約了艾美出去看電影。

> **Q** 進階查詢
>
> 即 ask someone out on a date，剛開始和某人約會，都會先約對方外出，所以 on a date 通常都省略，因為 out 已經涵蓋 out on a date 的意思了。

② **Don't give me that.**

我不相信你隨便說的話。

例 A: I don't care if I win the contest.

　 B: Don't give me that. This contest means everything to you.

A：是否贏得比賽，我並不在乎。

B：你隨便說說的吧，這個比賽對你來說意義重大。

③ **Don't make me laugh.**

別說笑了；別荒謬了。

例 A: I doubt your computer can run this game.

B: Don't make me laugh. It can run any game on the market.

A：我懷疑你的電腦跑得動這個遊戲。

B：別說笑了，市面上所有遊戲它都跑得動。

④ **in the mood**

有心情；有情緒

例 It's dinner time. What are you in the mood for?

晚餐時間到了，你想吃什麼呢？

⑤ **Cut it out.**

別鬧了。

例 Cut it out. Why are you bothering me?

別鬧了，你為什麼要煩我？

☑ 精挑句型

綠字部分為替換語詞，你也可以試著加上更多適當的替換字詞。

①

	afraid?
Or are you	scared?
	nervous?

要不然，你就是在害怕囉？／害怕囉？／緊張囉？

②

	mama's boy.
I'm not a	baby.
	coward.

我不是膽小鬼。／嬰兒。／懦夫。

③

	right now.
I'll go talk to her	in a second.
	when I'm ready.

我現在／馬上／準備好就去跟她說。

✎ Exercises 動手做

A 請由本單元的片語中挑選出適當者，填入下列空格。

1. A: Kevin _____ out yesterday.
   B: Fantastic!

2. A: But we're too little to climb the mountain.
   B: Don't _____ that. I know you can do it.

3. A: If you can't handle this case, I'll take it.
   B: _____ laugh. You know I'm the best person for the job.

4. A: Want to get a pizza?
   B: Nah, I'm not _____!

5. A: I love math class.
   B: _____ that. You hate math.

6. Are you _____ to take a walk?

7. _____ out. Please just leave me alone.

8. I want to _____ Carol _____, but I'm afraid she'll say no.

9. Don't _____. I could easily beat you at chess.

解答、中譯請見第 239 頁

Andrew's 精選對話 🎧 MP3 49

Two colleagues are at a bar. They're relaxing after a hard day at work.

Gary: I hear you've been seeing that girl in accounting. What's her name?

Burt: Vera. How'd you find out?

Gary: Let's just say a little birdie told me. So what's going on? Give me the lowdown.

Burt: There's not much to say yet.

Gary: I doubt that. Don't hold out on me, man. Is it serious?

Burt: Not really, but she did tell me something. Promise you won't tell anyone else.

Gary: Me? Impossible! Come on, spill the beans. Tell me, and the next round's on me.

Burt: OK. She said she went out with you once. And you took your mother and big sister with you. Plus, you wore a Mickey Mouse hat on the date.

Gary: Hah, hah. Very funny. You can buy your own drink.

翻譯

兩個同事在酒吧裡，在一整天的辛苦工作後，他們正在放鬆一下。

蓋瑞：我聽說你在跟會計部的那個女孩子交往，她叫什麼名字？

伯特：薇拉。你怎麼知道的？

蓋瑞：就當是**某個人告訴我的**。所以，你們進展得如何？**全都告訴我嘛**。

伯特：還沒有什麼可以說的。

蓋瑞：我不相信。別**對我有所隱瞞**，夥伴。這段關係是認真的嗎？

伯特：也不盡然，不過她確實告訴了我一些事。你得保證你不會告訴別人。

蓋瑞：我？不可能！好啦，**一五一十地說出來吧**。你如果告訴我，**下一輪酒就算我的**。

伯特：好。她說她有一次跟你出去，你帶了媽媽和姊姊一起去，還有，你約會時還戴了頂米老鼠的帽子。

蓋瑞：哈哈，很好笑，你付你自己的飲料錢吧。

🖋 進階解析

• you've been seeing that girl

即 you've been going out with that girl「你一直都在跟那個女孩見面；你一直都在跟那個女孩約會」；seeing someone 即「跟某人約會」的意思。

• How'd you find out?

即 How did you find out?「你是怎麼發現的？」的意思。

◉ 核心片語

① a little birdie told me
有人告訴我

例 A little birdie told me you're getting married.

有人告訴我說你要結婚了。

---

② Give me the lowdown.
全都告訴我；告訴我所有的事。

例 Give me the lowdown on your new job.

告訴我所有關於你新工作的事。

---

③ hold out on someone
對某人有所隱瞞或保留

例 Don't hold out on me. I know you've got more money than that.

你別對我有所隱瞞，我知道你有更多的錢。

> **Q 進階查詢**
>
> 拿了個東西卻不給某人看，某人知道有內情，卻不知道內情為何。所以這個片語就有「隱瞞某人不讓某人知道」的意思。

---

④ **spill the beans**

巨細靡遺地說出來；全盤托出

例 When are you going to spill the beans about what happened during your trip?

你什麼時候才要一五一十地告訴我你旅行時發生的事？

⑤ **something's on me**

我會付某物的錢

例 Dinner's on me. You paid last time.

晚餐我請客，你上次請過了。

☑ 精挑句型

綠字部分為替換語詞，你也可以試著加上更多適當的替換字詞。

①

I hear you've been	seeing that girl in accounting. going out with Jack. spending a lot of time with Pam.

我聽說你在跟會計部的那個女孩子交往。／在跟傑克約會。／花了很多時間和潘在一起。

②

There's	not much nothing very little	to say yet.

還沒有什麼／沒有什麼／沒有什麼可說的。

③

Promise You have to promise I need to make sure	you won't tell anyone else.

你得保證／你得保證／我要確定你不會告訴別人。

✎ Exercises 動手做

A 請由本單元的片語中挑選出適當者，填入下列空格。

1. A: Let's have lunch. I'll give _____ lowdown.
   B: Sure thing.

2. A: Come on, Jack. Spill _____ about the election.
   B: Sorry. No comment.

3. A: Don't hold _____ me. Tell me what you know.
   B: I'll say this. A little _____ me this company is about to see some major changes.

4. A: Order whatever you want. It's _____ me.
   B: Thanks!

B 選擇正確的字。

1. I just got a raise. Drinks are on/by me.

2. A little birdie told/sung me you got promoted.

3. I'm not holding/keeping out on you. I told you everything I know.

4. When are you going to say/give me the lowdown on what happened?

5. I couldn't keep quiet. I had to spill/drop the beans.

解答、中譯請見第 239 頁

Andrew's 精選對話

🎧 MP3 51

Pearl and Michael bring their children to visit one of their friends.

Pearl: Remember, children, to mind your p's and q's. The Appletons are very conservative people.

Davey: Are we going to eat here?

Pearl: Yes, but don't ask them about it. They'll tell you when it's time to eat.

Davey: Can we play?

Pearl: We'll ask them first. Remember to keep your hands to yourself.

Davey: Aw, it's just like being at school. What a drag.

Pearl: That's another thing. Keep a civil tongue in your mouth. I don't want you to embarrass me. If you do, you're in for it.

Davey: I'll be good. Can we go to the park on the way home?

Pearl: I think that can be arranged.

翻譯

珍珠和麥可帶了他們的孩子去拜訪一個朋友。

珍珠：記著，孩子們，**要注意禮貌**。雅柏頓家的人都很保守的喔。

戴維：我們會在這裡吃飯嗎？

珍珠：會啊，不過別問他們有關吃飯的事，他們會告訴你什麼時候要吃飯。

戴維：我們可以玩嗎？

珍珠：我們會先問他們，記得**別碰任何東西**。

戴維：噢，好像在學校一樣，**真不好玩**。

珍珠：還有一件事，**說話要有禮貌**，我不要你們讓我難堪，如果你們不聽話，你們就**麻煩大了**。

戴維：我會乖乖的。我們回家時可以去公園嗎？

珍珠：我想應該可以。

🖈 進階解析

• the Appletons

用 the +〔姓氏 + s〕指的是「姓……的這一家人」，例：the Johnsons「強森這一家人」、the Bennetts「班尼特這一家人」。

• just like + V-ing

意即「就像做……」，例：Taking a bus in Taipei is just like riding a roller coaster.「在台北搭公車就好像坐雲霄飛車一樣。」

• That's another thing.

即「另外有一件事要注意」。

• that can be arranged

並不是說「那件事可以被安排」，而是「應該可以；沒問題」的意思。

① **Mind your p's and q's.**

要注意禮貌。

例 Mind your p's and q's when you speak with your teacher.

你和老師說話時要注意禮貌。

---

② **Keep your hands to yourself.**

把手收好;別碰任何東西。

例 There are many valuable things here. Keep your hands to yourself.

這裡有很多有價值的東西,所以別碰任何東西。

> **Q** 進階查詢
>
> 把手收好在自己身上,就是教人不要用手亂碰東西,同理 Keep your opinion to yourself. 就是請對方「別把自己的意見說出來」,因為別人不會想聽。

③ What a drag.

好可惜；真是不幸。

例 A: The mall isn't open today.

B: What a drag. I need to do some shopping.

A：購物商場今天沒開。

B：運氣真背，我必須買些東西。

④ Keep a civil tongue in your mouth.

說話要尊敬有禮貌。

例 A: Mike said a dirty word today at school.

B: Don't be like him. Remember to keep a civil tongue in your mouth.

A：麥克今天在學校說了髒話。

B：別學他，記得說話要尊敬別人有禮貌。

⑤ in for it

有麻煩了

例 Uh-oh, the vase is broken. Now we're in for it.

喔哦，花瓶破了，現在我們真的麻煩大了。

綠字部分為替換語詞，你也可以試著加上更多適當的替換字詞。

①

The Appletons are very	conservative traditional old-fashioned	people.

雅柏頓家的人都很保守。／傳統。／守舊。

②

We'll ask them	first. beforehand. and see.

我們會先／事先／先問他們。

③

That's	another thing. another point. something else.

還有一件事。／一點。／一件事。

✐ Exercises 動手做

A 請由本單元的片語中挑選出適當者，填入下列空格。

1. A: This job's terrible.

   B: I know, but try to keep a _____ mouth when the boss gets back.

2. A: Our kids are the best. They know how to mind their _____.

   B: And when we go to someone's house, we keep our _____ ourselves.

3. Things are getting worse and worse. I think I'm in _____.

4. A: It looks like we'll be working late again today.

   B: What _____.

5. A: That's a stupid idea.

   B: You should keep _____ mouth.

6. Don't be so careless in class. You have to mind _____ around your teacher.

7. My car won't start, and I'm an hour late. Now I'm in _____.

8. A: The concert was cancelled.

   B: What _____.

9. Be careful, that's fragile! Try to keep _____.

解答、中譯請見第 240 頁

更多學習片語的竅門

☑ **流行娛樂**

　　讀完本書的片語後，看看有多少的片語出現在母語人士製作的音樂、電影、電視或其他型態的娛樂中。可能的話，試著將聽到的句子完整的寫下來。這可提供你一個更實用的情境，協助你對片語的理解。

☑ **網際網路**

　　瀏覽網路是學到新片語的好方法，也可以應用你在本書學到的片語知識。人們在網路上寫作時，都傾向使用非正式的口語表達，這是一種介於口語和標準書寫英語之間的文體，電子郵件在很多方面也有相同之處。

　　瀏覽一些討論區與網站，或是進入母語人士的聊天室，可以觀察到多樣的英文用法。你更可以加入並練習使用片語，在聊天室中你可以匿名，也不須和對方面對面，是一個很好的練習機會。

　　需注意的是，在聊天室中盡可能地表現自然，使用你最熟悉的英文，不要千方百計地想用高深的英文來表現自己。如果你不了解他人所說的，也沒關係。畢竟，聊天室裡通常會有許多人，你不一定得回覆所有的談話。

☑ **找出中文的對應說法**

　　這是個有趣的方式，可將你學到的英文片語和自己的語言作連結。不是所有的英文片語都有個完全對應的中文說法，但大部分的

片語應該有。

☑ 寫下簡短的對話

　　作為一個成功的語言學習者，重要的關鍵之一就是必須積極主動。除了大量閱讀之外，經常地寫作也很重要。藉由寫出自己的英文，可以增加你對所使用語言的了解。你可以藉此將新學到的字彙、片語、句型與你現有的英文基礎作整合。信不信由你，這個練習除了能改善你的寫作技巧，也可以增加你在聽、說、讀方面的能力。這是因為在「寫」這個產出的過程中，不但幫助你記憶，也加深了你對語言的理解。

　　以片語來說，我會建議寫個六至八行的簡短對話在筆記本上，該注意的重點是：不要擔心寫的句子不夠完美。這不是大學的論文，不會有嚴格的教授來打分數，也不會有人因為你將標點符號放錯地方而責備你。這個練習的目的不是讓你收集一堆完美的文章或對話，而是讓你去運用學到的語言、加深你對它們的認識。

　　此外，讓我告訴你們一個小秘密。母語人士寫的英文也會有錯。沒錯，從國中生到研究生都會犯錯。他們在寫作時，並不會擔心每個字母的位置是否正確。你也不應該擔心這個部分。不過，對於一些較正式的寫作，如商業書信和大學的論文，我建議你要做校訂，內容盡可能無誤。

　　下列是運用了一些片語所寫出的對話範例。

Doug: Flying overseas can be so frustrating. They won't let me change the date of my flight!

Frank: I know where you're coming from. Last year we took a trip to Europe, and we had a really hard time booking a flight.

Doug: I believe it. You know, these tickets almost put me in the poor house. But they still won't let me change the date.

Frank: Is it high season?

Doug: Maybe. Anyway, I think next year I'll take a trip locally and avoid the hassle.

Frank: I hear you.

道格　：搭飛機出國也能讓人覺得如此沮喪。他們不讓我更改飛機的日期！

法蘭克：我能了解。去年我們到歐洲旅行，機票非常難訂。

道格　：我相信。你知道嗎，這些機票花了我不少錢。但他們居然不讓我更改日期。

法蘭克：現在是旺季嗎！

道格　：也許吧。不管怎麼說，我想明年我要在當地旅遊就好，避免這些困擾。

法蘭克：我也有同感。

如果你願意，可以將對話中的片語列在對話下方，如下：

- I know where you're coming from. 我知道你的意思。
- put someone in the poor house 讓某人花很多錢
- I hear you. 我懂你的意思。

　　或者，你可以在未來的幾週或是幾個月的時間，試著使用書中所有的片語。使用一個片語後，就於書上作記號。如果有你喜歡的片語，就儘量地使用吧。你使用的次數愈多，就會用得愈自在，也記得愈清楚。

Chapter 7

Home 家庭

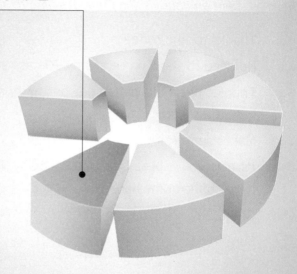

Andrew's 精選對話

MP3 53

Ben has spent an hour visiting Chris. It's time to say goodbye.

Ben: Thanks for the coffee.

Chris: No need to stand on ceremony. Mi casa su casa.

Ben: Thanks. Well, I'd better get on my horse, if I want to beat the traffic.

Chris: Makes sense.

Ben: I'll give you a buzz in a week or two. Next time we can have coffee at my house.

Chris: Great. Say hi to your wife for me.

Ben: Sure thing.

翻譯

班已經在克里斯家待了一個小時，該是說再見的時候了。

班　　：謝謝你招待的咖啡。

克里斯：沒必要那麼**客氣**，**我家隨時都歡迎你來**。

班　　：謝啦，我**該走了**，如果要**避開交通尖峰**的話。

克里斯：有道理。

班　　：我這一兩個禮拜**會打電話給你**，下一次我們可以在我家喝咖啡。

克里斯：好啊，幫我跟嫂夫人問好吧。

班　　：沒問題。

進階解析

• No need to

即 You don't need to，意為「你沒有必要……；……是不需要的」，例：No need to call the repairman. I can fix this myself.「沒必要找修理工人，我自己就能把這個修好。」

• Makes sense.

即 That makes sense.，省略掉 that，意思是「有道理」。

• Say hi to your wife for me.

常常我們會請對方幫我們問候某人，就可以用 Say hi to + someone + for me. 這個說法。

① **stand on ceremony**

舉止行為很客氣

例 We're all friends here. No one has to stand on ceremony.

我們在這裡的都是朋友，大家不需要客氣。

---

② **Mi casa su casa.**

我家隨時歡迎你來。

例 A: You've been an excellent host.

B: Mi casa su casa.

A：你是個很棒的主人。

B：我家隨時歡迎你來。

> **Q** 進階查詢
>
> 為西班牙語，即英文的 My house your house.，意思為「我家就是你家」，用來向對方表示「我家大門為你敞開，歡迎你隨時來玩」。

③ **get on one's horse**
要走了；離開

例 I'd love to stay longer, but I have to get on my horse.
我實在很想再多留一會兒，不過我真的得走了。

④ **beat the traffic**
避開交通尖峰時段

例 We'll leave before 4:00. That way we can beat the traffic.
我們會在四點以前離開，那樣我們就可以避開交通尖峰時段。

⑤ **give someone a buzz**
打電話給某人

例 Promise you'll give me a buzz soon.
答應我你很快就會打電話給我。

☑ 精挑句型

綠字部分為替換語詞，你也可以試著加上更多適當的替換字詞。

①

Thanks for I appreciate Many thanks for	the coffee.

謝謝／感謝／多謝你招待的咖啡。

②

Next time we can	have coffee eat dinner get together	at my house.

下一次我們可以在我家喝咖啡。／吃晚餐。／聚一聚。

③

Say hi Give my best Send my regards	to your wife for me.

幫我向嫂夫人問好。／問好。／致意。

✎ Exercises 動手做

A 請由本單元的片語中挑選出適當者，填入下列空格。

1. A: I'm late. I need to _____ horse.

    B: I understand. Remember, mi _____.

2. A: Are you almost done? I need to leave soon, so I can beat

    _____

    B: Yes, I'm almost done.

3. A: You've been a very gracious host.

    B: Please don't stand _____. And make sure to give

    _____ soon. I'd like to talk about this some

    more.

4. It's almost rush hour. If you don't leave now, you won't

    _____.

5. When we're settled in our hotel, I'll _____ buzz.

6. You're always so formal. There's no need to _____.

7. Now that we've taken care of business, I have to get

    _____.

8. Come back any time, Kimberley. Mi _____.

解答、中譯請見第 241 頁

Andrew's 精選對話

🎧 MP3 55

Carol is assembling a shelf she bought from a furniture store.

Phil: Carol, what are you doing? You're putting that part on backwards!

Carol: I am not. Anyway, I'll put together my shelf as I see fit.

Phil: Suit yourself, but don't come crying to me when it comes crashing down.

Carol: It's not going to come crashing down.

Phil: I think it will.

Carol: And what makes you such an expert?

Phil: My dad owns a hardware store.

Carol: For real?

Phil: For real. Take my word for it, that shelf will not stay standing.

Carol: Then I may need your help after all.

翻譯

卡蘿正在組裝一個她從家具店買回來的架子。

菲爾：卡蘿，妳在幹嘛？妳把那個部分裝反了！

卡蘿：我才沒有。怎樣，我就是要把它組成**我想要的樣子**。

菲爾：**隨妳的便吧**，只不過它塌了以後**別來向我哭訴**。

卡蘿：它才不會塌掉呢。

菲爾：我覺得它會。

卡蘿：還有，你憑什麼覺得你是個專家？

菲爾：我爸擁有一家賣五金器具的店。

卡蘿：**真的嗎**？

菲爾：真的。**相信我吧**，這個架子沒辦法站起來的。

卡蘿：那麼，畢竟我可能還是需要你的協助。

進階解析

• come crashing down

crash down 就是「崩塌下來」，口語中常會用到 come + V-ing 的說法來形容某個動作的氣勢，例：come tumbling down「垮下來」。

• What makes you such a/an + N

另一個類似的說法為：What makes you so + adj.?，意思是「你憑什麼認為你是個……的人？」，例：What makes you so perfect?「你憑什麼認為你自己很完美？」

• stay standing

stay + V-ing 就是「保持在……的狀態」。

① **as I see fit**
我喜歡的樣子

例 I'll run my business as I see fit.

我想把我的事業經營成我喜歡的樣子。

---

② **Suit yourself.**
隨你喜歡;隨你高興。

例 A: You go to the beach. I'll stay home.

B: Suit yourself.

A:你去海邊吧,我要留在家裡。

B:隨你高興。

---

③ **Don't come crying to me.**
別來向我抱怨。

例 Don't come crying to me when your plan fails.

你的計劃如果失敗可別來找我哭訴。

> **Q** 進階查詢
>
> 字面意思為「別來對著我哭」,表示我已經警告過你,而你不聽,將來如果有什麼後果發生,我可不想聽你對我說些後悔的話。

④ **for real**
   真的

   例 A: You got elected to be class president? For real?
   B: For real. I can't believe it myself!
   A：你被選為班長啦？真的嗎？
   B：真的，連我自己都不敢相信！

⑤ **Take my word for it.**
   相信我。

   例 Take my word for it. He's a dishonest merchant.
   相信我，他是個不誠實的商人。

綠字部分為替換語詞，你也可以試著加上更多適當的替換字詞。

①

Carol, what	are you doing? do you think you're doing? are you trying to do?

卡蘿，妳在幹嘛？／妳想妳在做什麼？／妳到底想做什麼？

②

It's not going to It won't It will never	come crashing down.

它才不會／它才不會／它永遠不會塌掉。

③

And	what makes you since when are you why do you think you're	such an expert?

還有，你憑什麼覺得你是／打從何時起你變成／你為什麼覺得你是個專家？

✏ Exercises 動手做

▼

A 請由本單元的片語中挑選出適當者，填入下列空格。

1. A: It's my website. I'll manage it _____.
   B: _____. I still think you should make a few changes.

2. Like I said, it's not a good investment. _____ me if you lose money.

3. A: Take my _____. You're taller than your sister now.
   B: For _____? Cool!

4. A: How can I make sure you're right?
   B: You can _____. I am right.

5. Believe me, your engine needs repairing. Don't _____ when your car breaks down.

6. You know I don't like to take orders. I'm going to do things _____.

7. A: All this good luck is hard to believe.
   B: It's _____. We are really lucky!

8. A: I think I'll take the black sweater.
   B: _____. I still think the green sweater looks better on you.

解答、中譯請見第 241 頁

Andrew's 精選對話

🎧 MP3 57

It's 4:30 P.M. on a Sunday afternoon. Guests are starting to leave a barbecue at Jack and Melissa's house.

Keith: It looks like the kids are all set to go, so we're going to take off.

Jack: So soon?

Keith: I'm afraid so. The kids have to finish their homework.

Jack: Oh, right. Tomorrow's Monday.

Keith: Right. Anyway, thanks for a great time. It's been fun.

Jack: Thanks. I'm glad you could come.

Keith: You and Melissa should come by our place for dinner some time.

Jack: I'd like that. Well, don't be a stranger.

Keith: We won't. So long.

Jack: Bye.

翻譯

星期日午後四點半，參加了傑克和美黎莎家的烤肉聚會後，客人們開始準備要離開了。

奇斯：看來孩子們都**準備好**要走，那我們就**離開了**。

傑克：這麼快？

奇斯：我想是吧，孩子們還得做完功課呢。

傑克：喔，對呀，明天是禮拜一。

奇斯：是啊，不過，還是很謝謝你的殷勤招待，我們**玩得很愉快**。

傑克：謝啦，我很高興你們能來。

奇斯：你跟美黎莎應該找個時間到我們家來吃晚飯。

傑克：我會很高興去的，那麼，**要經常來玩喔**。

奇斯：會的，**再見了**。

傑克：再見。

⌕ 進階解析

• It looks like + S + V

「看來……要……」之意，例：It looks like Jean really doesn't like the party at all.「看來珍真的一點也不喜歡這個舞會。」

• So soon?

暗示有「不要這麼快就……」的意思。

• I'm afraid so.

「恐怕是如此」，肯定的說法用來表示「我想事情就是如此」；否定的說法則為 I'm afraid not.「恐怕不是如此」。

• come by + somewhere

「到某處待一段時間」之意。

① **all set**

全都準備好

例 I think everybody's all set to begin.

我想大家已經準備好可以開始了。

---

② **take off**

離開

例 It's 5:00. Time to take off.

五點了,該走囉。

---

③ **It's been fun.**

玩得很愉快。

例 I have to say, it's been fun. We should do it again some time.

我得說我玩得很愉快。我們以後應該再做一次。

---

④ **Don't be a stranger.**

常常來玩。

例 You're welcome here any time. Don't be a stranger.

這裡任何時候都歡迎你，要常常來玩喔。

> **Q** 進階查詢
>
> 「別像個陌生人」，即希望對方別像個陌生人一樣都不來拜訪，
> 而要常常來造訪。

⑤ **So long.**

再見。

例 A: See you later, James.

B: So long.

A：回頭見，詹姆士。

B：再見。

綠字部分為替換語詞，你也可以試著加上更多適當的替換字詞。

①

It looks like the kids	are all set to go. want to leave. are getting tired.

看來孩子們都準備好要走了。／想離開了。／都累了。

②

Anyway, thanks for	a great time. having us over. inviting us.

不過，還是很謝謝你（的）殷勤招待。／邀請我們過來。／邀請我們。

③

I'm	glad happy thrilled	you could come.

我很高興／高興／驚訝你們能來。

✎ Exercises 動手做

A 請由本單元的片語中挑選出適當者，填入下列空格。

1. Well, I should take _____. It was great seeing you again.

2. See you later. Don't be _____.

3. A: _____ fun. We'll see you later.
   B: _____ long!

4. You're all _____. You can go home now.

5. Is everybody all _____?

6. A: I had a great time today.
   B: Yeah, it's been _____.

7. So _____, Pete. I'll see you later.

8. When did you want to _____ off?

9. Please don't be a _____. We should get together more often.

解答、中譯請見第 242 頁

Andrew's 精選對話

MP3 59

Patty stops by Hillary's house on a Sunday afternoon.

Hillary: Hi, Patty. Come on in. Please make yourself at home.

Patty: OK.

Hillary: Have a seat anywhere. There are some snacks over there. Help yourself.

Patty: Thanks. Where are you going?

Hillary: I need to check on some cookies I'm baking. They should be just about ready.

Patty: Can I lend a hand?

Hillary: No, no, just rest up for a minute. I'll be back in a jiff.

Patty: Holler if you need some help, OK?

Hillary: You bet.

【翻譯】

一個星期天的下午佩蒂到希拉蕊家拜訪。

希拉蕊：嗨，佩蒂，請進，請**別拘束當在自己家**一樣。

佩蒂　：好啊。

希拉蕊：隨便找個地方坐，那裡有些點心，**自己來**。

佩蒂　：謝謝。妳要去哪裡？

希拉蕊：我得看一下正在烤的餅乾，餅乾應該快好了。

佩蒂　：我可以**幫忙**嗎？

希拉蕊：不用了，妳先休息一下吧，我**一下子**就回來。

佩蒂　：妳如果需要幫忙就大聲叫我，好嗎？

希拉蕊：**一定會**。

✎ 進階解析

• Come on in.
「請進」之意。

• have a seat
「請坐」，在口語中常用。

• check on + N
「查看一下某事物」，看看某事物現在的狀況如何，例：check on the kids「看看孩子們的狀況」。

• holler
「吆喝」之意，和 shout 同義，都是指「大聲喊叫」。

① **Make yourself at home.**

當成是在自己家一樣。

例 A:I love your apartment.

B: Thank you. Please make yourself at home.

A：我好喜歡你的公寓。

B：謝謝，當成是在你自己家一樣吧。

② **Help yourself.**

自己來別客氣；自己動手吧。

例 Help yourself to whatever snacks and drinks you want.

想吃什麼點心和飲料請自己動手，別客氣。

③ **lend a hand**

幫忙某人

例 Mike needs help painting his house. A few of us are going to lend a hand.

麥克需要人幫他油漆他的房子，我們有些人要去幫他。

④ **in a jiff**

馬上；一下子；一會兒

例 Don't move. I'll return in a jiff.

別動，我馬上回來。

⑤ **You bet.**

一定；當然；絕對好的。

例 A: Are you excited about the concert?

B: You bet.

A：你對這個演唱會感到很興奮嗎？

B：當然。

> **Q** 進階查詢
>
> 字面之意為「你打賭」，意即你穩贏的，所以你可以打賭。因此引申出「你是對的」、「你說得沒錯」的意思。

☑ 精挑句型

綠字部分為替換語詞，你也可以試著加上更多適當的替換字詞。

①

Have a seat Sit down You can sit	anywhere.

隨便找個地方坐。／坐。／想坐哪裡都可以。

②

There are some snacks I put some snacks out Help yourself to the food and drinks	over there.

有些點心／我拿了些點心放／隨便用些點心或飲料，它們放在那裡。

③

Holler if you need	some help. a hand. any assistance.

你如果需要什麼幫忙／幫忙／任何協助就大聲叫我。

✎ **Exercises** 動手做

A 請由本單元的片語中挑選出適當者，填入下列空格。

1. A: Will we arrive soon?

   B: _____ bet. We'll be there in _____.

2. A: Do you have anything to drink, Dad?

   B: There's a lot in the refrigerator. Help _____.

3. A: I'm going to paint my house tomorrow. Do you have any spare time?

   B: Sure. I'd be happy to lend _____.

4. A: I told my friend Sue to make herself _____. She fell asleep on my couch!

   B: That's funny!

5. We've got cookies, brownies, and cake. Please help
   _____.

6. If you need me to lend _____, I'd be more than happy to help.

7. I'm so glad you could come by. Make _____.

8. A: Do you want to go to the movies with me?

   B: You _____!

9. A: Don't be long.

   B: I won't. I'll be back in _____.

解答、中譯請見第 243 頁

動手做解答 🔍 ✏️

Chapter 1 Day 01

A 1. B: out　2. A: this　B: again　3. A: up　4. B: driving at

B 1. at　2. straight　3. Get　4. Come　5. out

翻譯

A

1. A：慢一點，親愛的。

　　B：我把這些路都摸透了，沒有理由該慢下來。

2. A：你聽聽這個，蒂娜跟法比歐分手了，她現在跟查理在一起。

　　B：你說什麼？

3. A：你最好直接說，你是不是在看我的女朋友！

　　B：我發誓我沒有。

4. A：我覺得也許是我們進一步交往的時候了。

　　B：你到底想說些什麼？

B

1. 你說得不是很清楚，你到底想說些什麼？

2. 我表哥直接告訴我他犯法了。

3. 聽聽這個，我的股票這個星期飆漲了三成。

4. 再說一遍，你剛剛是說你要結婚了嗎？

5. 如果有誰完全了解棒球的話，那就是艾德了。

Chapter 1 Day 02

A 1. B: two of us　2. had time to breathe　3. B: the spirit

　　4. A: cakewalk　B: say

B 1. B: I'll　2. B: the　3. B: makes　4. cakewalk　5. had

翻譯

A

1. A：我不在乎新的流行。

   B：我也跟你一樣。

2. 我這個禮拜非常忙，忙到沒時間喘息了。

3. A：好吧，我想我會繼續嘗試。

   B：就是這個精神！

4. A：要變得既富有又成功不容易啊。

   B：我同意，那需要很努力地工作。

B

1. A：這蛋糕真好吃。

   B：我同意，我得向蒂娜要食譜。

2. A：好吧，我會再試一次。

   B：就是這種精神！

3. A：我好累，我想我再也走不動了。

   B：我跟你一樣，好難爬的山啊！

4. 瑪莉說學會使用那套程式不是件易事。

5. 自從我又開始做起全職的工作，我就十分地忙碌。

Chapter 1 | Day 03

A 1. B: born yesterday   2. B: you say   3. dig our own

   4. A: up and up B: You

B 1. B: Whatever   2. and   3. digging   4. B: don't   5. B: born

翻譯

A

1. A：你在買二手車前一定要仔細檢查。

   B：我知道，我又不是三歲小孩子。

2. A：玩撲克牌的話，我可以打敗你們所有人。

   B：隨你怎麼說，我窮得沒法向你挑戰。

3. 我們的提案要小心謹慎一點，免得找自己的麻煩。

4. A：如果他們所說屬實，我們就可以從這筆生意賺很多錢。

　　B：真的嗎？那太棒了。

B

1. A：我可以在一對一的比賽輕易打敗麥可喬丹。

　　B：隨你怎麼說吧。

2. 你確定這是個誠實的交易嗎？

3. 席拉說所有事情都在她的掌控中，不過我真擔心她是在自掘墳墓。

4. A：我八月就要結婚了。

　　B：真的嗎？

5. A：他有可能在騙你。

　　B：我又不是三歲小孩子，我已經想到那種可能性。

Chapter 1 **Day 04**

A 1. B: brother　2. A: on it　B: your horses　3. B: Right　4. B: worked up

B 1. B: brother　2. B: Right on　3. Step on　4. worked up

　　5. your horses

翻譯

A

1. A：這是我們最好的香檳。

　　B：我的天啊，這要花我一大筆錢了。

2. A：你不能走快點嗎？電影四點半就要開演了。

　　B：別急，吉姆，我們還有很多時間。

3. A：就快完成了。

　　B：太好了。

4. A：你知不知道我已經等了一個小時？

　　B：放輕鬆點，別激動，我有個很好的理由。

B

1. A：我剛得到一隻新的貓。

　　B：我的天，你已經有三隻貓了。

2. A：我們要去迪士尼樂園渡假。

B：好棒！一定會很好玩。

3. 公車來了，快一點。

4. 這只是個小問題，沒必要這麼激動吧。

5. 你能走慢一點嗎？我沒辦法走那麼快。

Chapter 1 | Day 05

A 1. A: our shoulders B: the ball   2. A: the sob story   3. B: patch things

    4. A: cover for

B 1. B: your shoulders   2. patch things   3. the sob story   4. cover for

    5. drop the

翻譯

A

1. A：這個案子的成敗全看我們的了。

   B：沒錯，所以我們不能搞砸。

2. A：別想讓我為你難過，我們就快到了。

   B：不過，我好累喔，我已經走一整天了。

3. A：都是他的錯。

   B：這次我不會去填補他的過失了。

4. A：你確定你明天可以幫我代班？

   B：沒問題。

B

1. A：所以，都看我的囉？

   B：我想是吧，都看你了。

2. 我們大吵了一架，我懷疑會有那麼容易和好。

3. 我不想再聽你的問題了，所以你省省那些賺人熱淚的故事吧。

4. 我們可以讓你休幾天假，不過你要找人代班。

5. 我保證我不會再搞砸了，這次我會把工作做好。

A 1. away with　2. You lucky; it made　3. A: goes　B: old, same old

B 1. got　2. B: old; old　3. with　4. dog　5. A: it

翻譯

A

1. 你應該知道你逃不掉的。

2. 你真好運，有了那些你在股市所賺的錢，你往後就不用愁了。

3. A：見到你真好，最近過得怎樣？

　B：還是老樣子，你呢？

B

1. 贏了這所有的錢後，你的生活就有著落了。

2. A：你好嗎？

　B：還是老樣子。

3. 我不覺得你會辦到。

4. 你真是好狗運啊，我從沒贏過任何東西，而你卻贏了一輛新車。

5. A：你好嗎，崔司？

　B：嗨，芙羅，我很好，那妳呢？

A 1. A: out of your hair　2. A: a long shot　3. Fancy　4. A: get
B: my fingers crossed　5. B: Fancy that　6. A: out of your hair
7. getting by　8. a long shot　9. your fingers crossed

翻譯

A

1. A：我知道你很忙，所以我不再煩你了。

　B：沒關係，跟你說話一直是我的榮幸。

2. A：你並沒有和我一樣快，連「接近」都談不上。

　B：我知道，你慢一點。

3. 太令人驚訝了，現在才兩點半，而我已經做好了所有的工作。

4. A：如果我沒得到那個工作，我不知道我要怎麼過活。

　 B：我會為你禱告祈求好運。

5. A：阿琳說她想當會計。

　 B：太令人驚訝了，我以為她不喜歡數學呢。

6. A：我應該別再打擾你了。

　 B：胡說，我很高興有你作伴的。

7. 人家說飯店業最近比較不景氣，你還過得去吧？

8. 比賽還沒完呢，連「接近」都談不上。

9. 他們就要抽出中獎人，祈禱你有好運吧。

Chapter 2 Day 08

Ⓐ 1. A: got it off my　B: come off　2. B: could kill　3. A: a breather
　　4. B: have it

Ⓑ 1. B: it　2. chest　3. B: kill　4. take　5. as

【翻譯】

Ⓐ

1. A：我想說那些話已經很久了，我很高興我終於一吐為快。

　 B：你知道，你給人的感覺很強悍，不過事實上，你卻是非常敏感的。

2. A：我好餓。

　 B：我也是，我好想吃墨西哥菜。

3. A：你等一下想休息一下嗎？

　 B：好主意。

4. A：我剛想到一個很棒的計劃。

　 B：說來聽聽看。

Ⓑ

1. A：我有好消息！

　 B：說來聽聽。

2. 我得把這件事說出來，所以請聽我說。

3. A：我好餓。

　　B：我也是，我好想吃比薩。

4. 我們沒有時間小歇一會兒。

5. 凱蒂的穿著和談吐的樣子顯得她非常保守。

Chapter 2　Day 09

A 1. A: to put you　B: my share of　　2. A: is me　B: I can　　3. owe you

　　　4. owe you one　　5. my share of　　6. put you out　　7. can relate

　　　8. is me

翻譯

A

1. A：謝謝你幫我架好發電機，好鄰居，很抱歉增添你的麻煩。

　　B：不客氣，我也有過這種電機的麻煩。

2. A：這裡就是我家了，再次謝謝你。

　　B：別客氣，我以前也請過很多人載我回家，所以我能理解。

3. A：感謝你幫我準備化學考試，我欠你個人情。

　　B：我很高興能幫上忙。

4. 真是感謝你借車給我，我欠你一個人情。

5. A：我花園裡的雜草真多！

　　B：也許我幫得上忙，我以前也有處理雜草的麻煩。

6. A：我如果載你回家，我就會錯過電視轉播的籃球賽了。

　　B：我真的很抱歉給你添麻煩，不過你是我最後的希望了。

7. A：你懂我在說什麼嗎？

　　B：當然懂，我也有過類似的情形，我能了解你的狀況。

8. 這裡就是我家了，你可以讓我在路口下車。

Chapter 2　Day 10

A 1. of the loop　　2. black and white　　3. for the　　4. A: me in　B: for you

B 1. and   2. for   3. fill   4. you   5. loop

翻譯

A

1. 你不知道哈金結婚了嗎？你真的在狀況外。

2. 我們都同意合約裡所寫的，白紙黑字清清楚楚的寫在那兒。

3. 事件已經惡化，大火延燒已經失去控制。

4. A：我下個禮拜回來時，希望你們能詳細地告訴我課程內容，我真怕我的
   進度落後。

   B：我能體會你的感覺，一個禮拜後想要趕上進度是蠻難的。

   C：說得是！

B

1. 規範白紙黑字寫得很清楚。

2. 他的新朋友影響了他，讓他愈變愈糟。

3. 我還是需要你告訴我會議的細節。

4. 我真的替你感到很難過，但我不知道能怎麼幫你。

5. 由於你已經脫節了，你根本不知道發生了什麼事。

Chapter 3 Day 11

A 1. B: good one   2. A: the music B: me some slack
   3. A: a soul B: the point

B 1. a   2. slack   3. soul   4. face   5. point

翻譯

A

1. A：我該走了，再見。

   B：祝你愉快。

2. A：小心點，如果你弄壞了什麼東西，你得自嚐苦果。

   B：別對我這麼嚴格，我沒弄壞過什麼東西。

3. A：我知道有個錯誤，不過如果你不說，我也不會告訴任何人。

B：你沒搞清楚重點吧，我們的責任就是把事情做好。

B

1. 祝你愉快。
2. 可以拜託你別對我這麼嚴格嗎？
3. 就像我說過的，我不會告訴任何人。
4. 最後，每個罪犯都會自食其果。
5. 你還是沒抓住重點，我會再次解釋我的意思。

Chapter 3 Day 12

A 1. A: a sport   B: a good   2. B: give   3. B: How do you
   4. B: we go again   5. B: again   6. B: sport   7. give   8. B: figure
   9. That's

翻譯

A

1. A：跟我們去露營吧，很好玩的，一起去嘛。
   B：很好玩嗎？那可真好笑。我們上次去露營回來後我整整酸痛了一個禮拜。
2. A：好啦！我們買吧！
   B：好吧，我都聽你的。
3. A：你看，這真是筆好交易。
   B：你這想法哪兒來的？在我看來一點都不好。
4. A：我需要你加班。
   B：又來了，每個禮拜都發生同樣的事。
5. A：大家跟著我。
   B：又來了。
6. A：不過我不喜歡唱歌。
   B：一起來嘛，很好玩喔。
7. 不，我不會同意你的計畫，我拒絕加入。
8. A：我們應該會在五個小時內到達那裡。

B：你那個想法哪來的？通常最少要花七個小時的。

9. 那個笑話真好笑，我需要好好笑一笑。

Ⓐ 1. A: have in B: put me in the poor house 2. A: my head 3. you right
   4. up your alley 5. right 6. mind 7. over 8. poor 9. alley

翻譯

Ⓐ

1. A：你心裡想要的是什麼樣的車？
   B：一輛好車，只要它不會讓我破產。
2. A：今天教授所講的我都無法理解。
   B：我也是。
3. 有關這輛車，你可以相信我。就像我說的，我不會讓你吃虧的。
4. A：這個專案蠻適合你的。
   B：它是在我的專業領域內。
5. 你可以相信我，我會公平對待你的。
6. 野餐聽起來好像很好玩，你想去哪裡野餐呢？
7. 你聽得懂她在說什麼嗎？我完全無法理解。
8. 好吧，我會給你打個折扣，我不想害你破產。
9. 電視上有個有關於鳥類的節目，那蠻適合你的。

Ⓐ 1. leave you to 2. A: brings you here B: give you a hand
   3. A: a fright B: a matter of fact 4. fright 5. matter 6. leave
   7. brings 8. hand

翻譯

Ⓐ

1. 聽著，我知道你有很多事要做，所以我就讓你繼續忙你的事了。

2. A：查爾斯・菲爾德，什麼風把你吹來了？

　　B：我聽說你們需要幫忙，我是來助你們一臂之力的。

3. A：從樓梯上跌下來真的嚇了我一跳。

　　B：事實上，你完全健康。

4. 拜託別那樣嚇我，你真的嚇到我了。

5. A：你有丹妮絲的電話號碼嗎？

　　B：事實上，我有。

6. 我可以看得出來我耽誤了你的工作，所以我就讓你繼續工作吧。

7. 禮拜天你怎麼會來這裡呢？

8. 我想去，不過我得幫我兄弟做些事。

Chapter 4 Day 15

Ⓐ 1. A: and for all　B: it anymore　2. a grip　3. a fit　4. your best shot

Ⓑ 1. B: Get　2. have　3. all　4. take　5. B: Give

翻譯

Ⓐ

1. A：我們終於要一勞永逸地修好這條道路了。

　　B：這個噪音搞得我抓狂，我再也受不了了。

2. 冷靜一點，事情沒有看起來的那麼糟。

3. 我撞爛我男朋友的車時，他發脾氣了。

4. A：盡力而為，我們相信你能贏的。

　　B：謝謝。

Ⓑ

1. A：你開太快了！

　　B：冷靜一點，我沒超速。

2. 沒理由為了這麼小的問題而發脾氣的。

3. 這些雜草一直破壞我的花園，我得想個辦法一勞永逸地解決它們。

4. A：你要去哪裡？你幹嘛下車？

　　B：我們已經塞在車陣中兩個小時，我再也受不了了，我要用走的！

5. A：這次打籃球我要打敗你。

  B：你盡力而為吧。

A 1. B: buy it　2. A: holds barred　B: here　3. B: me a　4. B: Give me a

B 1. barred　2. buy　3. giving　4. Give　5. B: here

翻譯

A

1. A：這個一點也不會痛。

  B：我不相信，那些電鑽一直都讓人覺得痛的。

2. A：我們那些競爭對手不擇手段地打擊我們，我想你們一定都同意這些行動是必要的。

  B：我同意。

3. A：我是你女兒的……嗯，讀書夥伴。

  B：別騙我，我知道你是她的新男朋友。

4. A：我保證我很快就會去剪頭髮。

  B：別可笑了，你已經那樣說好幾個禮拜了。

B

1. 這些打者不擇手段地攻擊對方。

2. 我才不管他有什麼證據，我不會相信的。

3. 我不會誆騙你的，我所說的都是認真的。

4. 你別可笑了，你知道意外不是那樣發生的。

5. A：我們必須使上大學就讀更容易負擔得起。

  B：我有同感。

A 1. is on the line　2. A: it quits　B: you there　3. B: sure　4. A: you later

  5. B: Catch you later　6. neck is on the line　7. B: For sure

8. call it quits　9. B: with you there

A

1. 強森，我希望你了解，如果你搞砸了，你得負起全責。

2. A：我覺得我們不該還沒完成就停工了。

　　B：我同意，我們得在今天完成。

3. A：這個蛋糕會很棒的。

　　B：當然！你的烹飪技術一直都是很好的。

4. A：我要回家了，再見。

　　B：再見。

5. A：再見，彼得。

　　B：再見，提摩西。

6. 請小心一點，因為這是我朋友的房子。如果你打壞了任何東西，我可是要負責的。

7. A：這張 CD 很棒對不對？

　　B：當然，這是他們到目前為止最好的 CD。

8. 你已經輸了很多錢，你該歇手了。

9. A：我想我們該去另一個俱樂部。

　　B：我同意，這裡到處都是煙。

Chapter 5 Day 18

A 1. B: Get out　2. A: my string　B: it easy　3. A: happening　B: treat

　　4. easy　5. treat　6. jerking　7. happening　8. out

翻譯

A

1. A：這件洋裝要三百元。

　　B：我不相信，我以為它有折扣。

2. A：你在開我玩笑嗎？你真的要辭掉你的工作？

B：放輕鬆點，我還沒確定呢。

3. A：嗨，弗瑞德，你在幹嘛？

　　B：早啊，傑得，我正想帶著我們兩家出去吃晚飯，我請客。

4. 放輕鬆，我只是開個玩笑而已。

5. 晚飯後，我帶你們大家出去吃冰淇淋，我請客。

6. 我知道你在尋我開心。

7. 你們大家在幹嘛呀？

8. 你剛升為經理嗎？我不相信。

Chapter 5　Day 19

Ａ 1. A: where you're coming　2. B: said than done　3. B: No　C: a trip
　　4. B: Beats　5. B: way　6. B: Beats　7. B: trip　8. easier
　　9. B: coming

翻譯

Ａ

1. A：這個東西的價格一直漲。

　　B：我知道你的意思。

2. A：你該戒掉喝咖啡了。

　　B：哈！那真是說的比做的容易。

3. A：看這裡，我以前很受女孩們歡迎的。

　　B：不可能吧！那是你嗎？

　　C：哇，真令人驚訝，你變了很多。

4. A：你覺得這些夢有什麼意義？

　　B：問倒我了。

5. A：我繼承了五萬美金。

　　B：你說真的嗎？

6. A：他們的新 CD 什麼時候發行？

　　B：問倒我了。

7. A：你能相信發生了什麼事嗎？

B：是啊，那真令人驚訝。

8. 要在今天把這些全部完成真是說的比做的容易啊。

9. A：不過我真的不想搬。

B：我知道你的意思。

Chapter 5 Day 20

A 1. A: drop B: a piece of my mind   2. A: your temper

　3. A: ticked B: a scene   4. B: drop it   5. ticked off   6. his temper

　7. make a scene   8. B: him a piece of my mind

翻譯

A

1. 我覺得你還是別說了，不然你在工作上可能會遇到麻煩。

　B：我不管，我要告訴老闆我真正的想法。

2. A：人家說你會為些小事情發脾氣，是真的嗎？

　B：我想是真的吧，我很容易生氣。

3. A：我生氣了，你得學個教訓。

　B：如果你要把場面弄得這麼尷尬，沒關係，我奉陪。

4. A：我們再多談談這件事。

　B：不了，而且如果你不再說下去，我會很感激的。

5. 當我看到史提夫憤怒的表情，我知道他生氣了。

6. 我告訴泰勒裘說了什麼時，他就發脾氣了。

7. 大家都在看我們，你為什麼一定要把場面弄得這麼尷尬？

8. A：你不該讓克拉瑪用那種態度跟你講話。

　B：你說得對，下次我看到他，我會告訴他我心裡真正的想法。

Chapter 5 Day 21

A 1. the top; sense into you   2. B: advertise it to

　3. A: back me B: you insist

B 1. sense 2. back 3. over 4. advertise 5. insist

翻譯

A

1. 你這是什麼意思？說我太過分！我一定要和你說清楚，即使那是我最後能做的事。

2. A：嘿，你的新髮型看起來很棒。

   B：我希望你不會到處宣揚。

3. A：我跟強森說話時，別忘了支持我，我需要你的支持。

   B：如果你堅持的話，我希望你知道自己在做些什麼。

B

1. 你能幫我說服我女兒讓她清醒點嗎？

2. 怎麼會沒有人支持我？

3. 很多評論家都覺得那個提案太過火了。

4. 別告訴任何人，我不想讓全世界的人都知道。

5. 如果你堅持的話，我會去做。只不過我並不是很樂意去做它。

Chapter 6 Day 22

A 1. A: a long time 2. A: been treating you B: complain 3. A: me crazy
   4. B: about time
B 1. about 2. long 3. drives 4. can't 5. been

翻譯

A

1. A：嗨，安妮，好久不見。

   B：是啊，我已經四、五年沒看到你了。

2. A：嗨，菲爾，近來好嗎？

   B：喔，不錯啊，諸事順利。

3. A：可不可以拜託你別再說些愚蠢的笑話了，你快讓我抓狂了。

   B：對不起，我以為你喜歡我說的笑話。

4. A：你終於升遷了。

　　B：是啊，也該是時候了，我已經等了好多年了。

B

1. 你終於結婚啦？該是時候了。

2. 我好高興看到你，真的好久不見了。

3. 住在都市裡有時候真的會讓我抓狂。

4. A：你好嗎？

　　B：還不錯。

5. 歡迎您來參加舞會，李德先生，近來好嗎？

Chapter 6　Day 23

A　1. A: mop up the floor　B: my own business　2. get something straight

　　　3. B: what army　C: full of hot　4. B: and what army

　　　5. mop up the floor with　6. mind my own business

　　　7. get something straight　8. full of hot air

翻譯

A

1. A：我要把你痛扁一頓。

　　B：唉唷！今後，我最好別再管閒事了。

2. 所以他就說：「我們把話說清楚，我是老闆。」然後我就說：「再也不是了，我辭職。」

3. A：我可以痛毆任何笨到把我惹火的人。

　　B：就憑你嗎？

　　C：那個傢伙在虛張聲勢吧。

4. A：住手，不然我要把你揍扁。

　　B：就憑你嗎？

5. 那傢伙好巨大，他可以把我們揍扁。

6. 不，我不會不管，我想知道發生了什麼事。

7. 我們把話說清楚，在這裡我是老闆。

8. 艾倫只是虛張聲勢而已，他連一隻蒼蠅都不會傷害。

Chapter 6 Day 24

A A: asked me　2. B: give me　3. B: Don't make me　4. B: in the mood
　5. B: Don't give me　6. in the mood　7. Cut it　8. ask; out
　9. make me laugh

翻譯

A

1. A：凱文昨天約我出去。
　B：那太棒了。
2. A：我們還太小，沒辦法爬山。
　B：別說那些廢話，我知道你們辦得到。
3. A：如果你無法處理那個案子，我會接下來。
　B：你別逗我笑了，你明知道我是這個工作最好的人選。
4. A：要來塊比薩嗎？
　B：不了，沒那個心情。
5. A：我喜歡數學課。
　B：別胡說了，你明明很討厭數學的。
6. 你有心情去散個步嗎？
7. 別鬧了，拜託你讓我獨處。
8. 我想約卡蘿出去，不過我很怕她會拒絕。
9. 別逗我笑了，在下棋方面我可以輕易地打敗你。

Chapter 6 Day 25

A 1. A: you the　2. A: the beans　3. A: out on　B: birdie told　4. A: on
B 1. on　2. told　3. holding　4. give　5. spill

翻譯

A

1. A：我們去吃午餐吧，我會全部告訴你。

   B：好啊。

2. A：好啦，傑克，全盤托出有關選舉的事。

   B：很抱歉，無可奉告。

3. A：別對我有所隱瞞，告訴我你知道些什麼？

   B：我會說，有人告訴我，這家公司將有重大改變。

4. A：想點什麼都可以，全算我的。

   B：謝謝。

B

1. 我剛加薪了，飲料錢算我的。

2. 有人告訴我，你升遷了。

3. 我並沒有對你有所隱瞞，我告訴你所有我知道的事了。

4. 你什麼時候才要告訴我所有發生的事？

5. 我無法保持靜默，我必須全盤托出。

Chapter 6 Day 26

A 1. B: civil tongue in your　2. A: p's and q's　B: hands to　3. for it

   4. B: a drag　5. B: a civil tongue in your　6. your p's and q's

   7. for it　8. B: a drag　9. your hands to yourself

翻譯

A

1. A：這工作真糟。

   B：我知道，不過老闆回來時講話可要有禮貌。

2. A：我們的孩子最棒了。他們知道要有禮貌。

   B：而且我們去別人家時，我們不會亂碰人家的東西。

3. 事情愈變愈糟了，我想我麻煩大了。

4. A：看來我們今天又要加班了。

   B：真不幸。

5. A：那是個蠢主意。

B：你講話應該尊重別人。

6. 上課不要漫不經心，在老師旁邊要有禮貌。

7. 我的車發不動，而且我還遲到了一個小時，現在我真的麻煩大了。

8. A：演唱會取消了。

B：好可惜。

9. 小心啊，那是個易碎品，試著別碰任何東西。

Chapter 7 Day 27

A 1. A: get on my B: casa su casa   2. A: the traffic

3. B: on ceremony; me a buzz   4. beat the traffic   5. give you a

6. stand on ceremony   7. on my horse   8. casa su casa

翻譯

A

1. A：我遲到了，我得走了。

B：我了解，記著，我家隨時歡迎你來。

2. A：你快好了吧？我得趕快離開了，這樣才可以避開交通尖峰時段。

B：是啊，就快好了。

3. A：你是個很好的主人。

B：請別這麼客氣，還有，你一定要趕快給我打個電話，我想再多談談這件事。

4. 尖峰時段就快到了，如果你不現在離開，你就避不開壅塞的交通。

5. 等我們在飯店安頓好了，我就給你個電話。

6. 你總是這麼客套，不需要客氣的。

7. 由於我們有生意要照顧，我得離開了。

8. 隨時再來，金柏莉，我家隨時歡迎你來。

Chapter 7 Day 28

A 1. A: as I see fit B: Suit yourself   2. Don't come crying to

3. A: word for it　B: real　　4. B: take my word for it　　5. come crying to me

6. as I see fit　　7. for real　　8. B: Suit yourself

翻譯

A

1. A：這是我的網站，我想把它弄成我喜歡的樣子。

　 B：隨你高興，我還是覺得你該做些修改。

2. 就像我之前所說的，這不是個好投資。如果你賠了錢，別來向我哭訴。

3. A：相信我，你現在比你姊姊高了。

　 B：真的嗎？好棒！

4. A：我怎能確定你是對的？

　 B：你可以相信我，我是對的。

5. 相信我，你的引擎需要修理了，要是你的車故障了，你可別來向我抱怨。

6. 你知道我不喜歡接受指令，我就做我想做的。

7. A：這麼好的運氣真叫人難以相信。

　 B：是真的，我們真的很幸運！

8. A：我想我還是拿這件黑色毛衣。

　 B：你喜歡就好，我還是覺得你穿綠色的毛衣比較好看。

Chapter 7　Day 29

A　1. off　　2. a stranger　　3. A: It's been　B: So　　4. set　　5. set　　6. B: fun

7. long　　8. take　　9. stranger

翻譯

A

1. 我該走了，很高興再見到你。

2. 再見，常常來玩喔。

3. A：我們玩得很愉快，再見了。

　 B：再見！

4. 你都準備好了，你現在可以回家了。

5. 大家都準備好了嗎？

6. A：我今天玩得很愉快。

    B：是啊，是很好玩。

7. 再見，彼得，待會兒見。

8. 你想要什麼時候離開？

9. 請常常來玩，我們應該更常聚聚。

Chapter 7 | Day 30

A 1. B: You; a jiff　2. B: yourself　3. B: a hand　4. A: at home
    5. yourself　6. a hand　7. yourself at home　8. B: bet　9. B: a jiff

翻譯

A

1. A：我們快要到了嗎？

    B：你說對了，我們再一下子就到了。

2. A：爸，你這裡有什麼可以喝的東西嗎？

    B：冰箱裡有一大堆，自己動手吧。

3. A：我明天要油漆我的房子，你有空嗎？

    B：當然有空，我很高興能幫忙。

4. A：我告訴我朋友蘇別客氣，當成在自己家一樣，她就在我的沙發上睡著了。

    B：真有趣。

5. 我們有餅乾、布朗尼、蛋糕，請自己動手別客氣。

6. 你如果需要我的協助，我會很樂意幫忙的。

7. 我好高興你能來，請當成在自己家一樣。

8. A：你想跟我去看電影嗎？

    B：當然。

9. A：別耽擱太久。

    B：不會的，我一下子就回來。

國家圖書館出版品預行編目資料

多角建構英文片語 / 白安竹作；-- 初版. -- 臺北市：
　貝塔，2014. 11
　　面：　公分
　　ISBN: 978-957-729-978-9（平裝）
　1. 英語　2. 慣用語

805.123　　　　　　　　　　　　　　　　103020840

多角建構英文片語

作　　者 / 白安竹
執行編輯 / 朱慧瑛

出　　版 / 貝塔出版有限公司
地　　址 / 台北市 100 館前路 12 號 11 樓
電　　話 / (02) 2314-2525
傳　　真 / (02) 2312-3535
客服專線 / (02) 2314-3535
客服信箱 / btservice@betamedia.com.tw
郵撥帳號 / 19493777
帳戶名稱 / 貝塔出版有限公司

總 經 銷 / 時報文化出版企業股份有限公司
地　　址 / 桃園縣龜山鄉萬壽路二段 351 號
電　　話 / (02) 2306-6842

出版日期 / 2015 年 1 月初版一刷
定　　價 / 350 元
Ｉ Ｓ Ｂ Ｎ / 978-957-729-978-9

貝塔網址：www.betamedia.com.tw